TRIANGLES

OF

DECEPTION

III

Published by R & R Publishing, LLC

Cover photo and design by K and T Graphics

Editing by Latoya Carter Q

PUBLISHER'S NOTE

This book is a work of fiction. Names, characters, places, incidents or any resemblances to an actual person, business or localizes entirely coincidental are the product of the authors imagination.

Bulk quantities are available for distribution. Please contact R&R Publishing, LLC, P.O. Box 25962, Richmond, VA 23260. Telephone: 804-316-5792

ISBN: 9780997358858

Acknowledgments

This last book I want to dedicate to my cousin Brandy. It saddens me to know that you won't get to read the last book of this series. After all, you practically help me write the storyline. I made it my mission to finish this book this year, so this is definitely all for you!

Thanks to everyone that has kept me going with writing this last. You guys have been awesome. I wish I could personally thank each and every one that has purchased my book. Just know and understand I appreciate every ounce of support that I have received. You guys definitely keep me going.

Thank you to my husband that stayed up countless nights to listen to my ideas, to brainstorm and to support. I couldn't have done this without you.

To Latoya, you have been there since the first book offering your assistance in more ways than anyone could imagine. Thank you for being a great friend.

Brian

Things were different without him. All my life I thought needed him as my crutch, in reality, I didn't need him. I was running things by myself. This was probably the best thing that could have happened in my life. I just didn't think it would happen this way. His role in the company was minimal compared to mine. He was just a thug from the streets that had money. I made this company what is now. Without his money, there wouldn't be a company, but without me there wouldn't be a company still running. The majority of the time, he had no knowledge of anything that was happening in meetings, revenue, returns, or investments. He just wanted to be on the straight and narrow so bad. I had to make him feel important. He thinks he really made Shawna's company go bankrupt. That was me, all me. I was the one that was laundering money. I fixed the numbers. I had the money going into an off shore account.

The best part is that I now get to run this company by myself with the help of Shawna. I desperately want Shawna to sell her portion of the company. That way Lisa and I can run the company together. We are getting married in a few months. Terrance would have been my best man. Our personal friendship suffered over the past few months leading up to his death. I didn't approve of his lifestyle. I definitely felt a lot different about him after his trial. No one would have never known about Terrance. He did a great job of keeping his lifestyle a secret.

Lisa

I felt so bad for Shawna, but she had been so lucky to have Terrance all these years. I was always secretly jealous of Shawna and everything she had. I knew she worked for everything she had, but here I was always over here struggling to make ends meet. No, I didn't have kids, it was just me and Brian. We had been a couple for almost a decade. He finally popped the question six months ago. While Terrance had popped the question ten years ago. I finally was going to get to live the life that Shawna always had. Shawna was so resilient. She always seemed to bounce back. I just wanted her to struggle just once in her life. When she did, I wouldn't have wished that pain on my worst enemy. I knew I had to be there for her. Then she told me she was pregnant and I was jealous all over again. I was pregnant twice with Brian's baby and lost them both. Shawna was so wrapped up with her own life, I never even shared the news with her. Why was I the one that to struggle?

I felt bad because I was the one that told Tonya the location of the baby shower. I didn't know things were going to end up the way that they did. I was just hoping that Shawna got hurt in the process, not Terrance. I felt like I was always a good friend to Shawna, but I was a doormat to her. I was the godmother to her oldest son and now her daughter. She was always so dismissive of me. I needed Shawna to suffer like I did. I saw the perfect opportunity. I was relieved when they didn't

3

have to call me as a witness to testify at Tonya's trial. Shawna would have really been upset. I was a witness because I was following her that day. I wanted to get proof that she was cheating on Terrance. I didn't anticipate Tonya to show up and try to kill her though. I knew I had an ally. But I only could use her without her knowing.

It has been six months since the passing of Terrance. Shawna has still been a thorn in our side because she owns part of the company Brian runs. Terrance knew nothing, but Shawna knows everything. This could really be a headache if she is involved in our company. We need her gone.

Shawna

It has been six months to the date that Terrance passed away. I was so busy taking care of Morgan and TJ that I was distracted. There was not a moment that went by that I didn't think of him. The older Morgan got the more she looked like Jamie. There was no denying it. But I wasn't going to call him and tell him. My life was perfectly fine. I worked from home after maternity leave. I found that it was easier for me to work from home. I had just put Morgan down to sleep when my doorbell rang. Damnit, they bet not wake up Morgan.

"Mrs. James?"

"Yes." I was annoyed.

"My name is Detective Lawrence. Do you mind if I come in for a minute?"

"Um sure." I was confused.

"Mrs. James, we have continued to investigate your husband's death. We retrieved two bullets from the crime scene."

"Why are you still investigating? I thought this was an open and shut case. You know who did it! She is in the psych hospital!"

"No Mrs. James, the second bullet came from a separate gun."

"What?" I sat down. I felt nauseous.

"This mean that there were two shooters. The bullet that hit your husband is not the same bullet that we retrieved that the crime scene."

This didn't make sense. I was so sure that Tonya did this. Who else would have wanted Terrance dead? Terrance acted pretty paranoid before his death, I just thought that he was scared of losing me. I'm kicking myself for feeling like I didn't know enough about Terrance and his past. This wasn't supposed to be an investigation. This was supposed to end with Tonya going to jail or being locked up in a mental hospital for the rest of her life.

"What are the next steps?"

"We will continue our investigation and we will let you know when we have something else. Until then, be safe."

When Detective Lawrence left, my thoughts began to run wild. What if they were coming for me next? Did they only want Terrance? I was allowing my paranoia to get the best of me. If they wanted me, I'd be dead by now.

Tonya

Today was the day that I finally left this crazy place. I called Jamie to pick me up. I felt better than I ever felt. I looked better than I ever looked. The last year of my life has been pure hell. I felt like I was in jail. They told me when I could eat, sleep. The only thing I had control of was when I had to shit. The doctor said that I needed to stay on medications. They made me feel sleepy most days, but the good outweighed the bad.

I couldn't believe Terrance was dead. I also didn't believe I killed him either. Shawna was the bitch that should have been dead. My therapist said that I was obsessed with Shawna. She said that I needed to get past the everything that has happened and that none of it was her fault. I had to remember it wasn't Shawna's fault. It really was Terrance's fault. I did not have a real reason to hate Shawna. I just hated that Terrance was still married to her. I hated the fact that she had everything that I wanted. I hated that it was taken all from me, it was supposed to be us together. I heard that Shawna had her baby. I didn't know if I was to the point of forgiveness yet. However, I have gotten to a point of moving forward. I wanted to move out of state and start all over, somewhere like New York or Virginia. I needed to get out of Maryland. There weren't any good memories here. Jamie wanted me to come live with him and his boyfriend while I get my shit together. I didn't want to, but I didn't have a place to go. But my bank account was looking nice. I stacked all of the money that Terrance gave me, and the money that my ex-husband is paying me. I have a little over $500,000 in my account. It hasn't been touched in a while. I should go shopping. I felt good about myself. I was going to go shopping today. I wanted to eat at nice restaurant. I could wait to be out. This crazy place was a little better than jail.

I saw Jamie walk in. He looked like a million bucks. I went into hug him. His hugs were always so warm. I felt like I needed it.

"Ms. Billiard." The nurse approached the both of us.

"Yes."

"We just need to go over a few things with Jamie before you are discharged."

"Sure"

"We have your medications listed here. There are only two. Please remember to take them. If she has any thoughts of harming herself or other people, please do not ignore the signs. Please call her therapist, or bring her back here. Ms. Billiard is very unstable without her medications. This is the number to her therapist, visits are already scheduled for the next month. If you have any other questions, please do not hesitate to contact us."

8

"The nurse made it sound like I am crazy." I nudged Jamie and faked a laugh.

Jamie looked at me with a serious look and reminded me the seriousness of everything. The nurse handed me my things, and told me I was free to go. Other than walking around the hospital, I hadn't been outside in almost nine months. They were afraid that I was going to run. I had nowhere to go, so I didn't want to run. I just wanted to smell the outside.

"How are you, Tonya?" Jamie broke the ice.

"I'm good. I feel better since being back on my medications."

"I'm glad to hear that. Before we get home, I have something that I need to tell you. You may not like it. I would rather you find it out from me than anyone else."

I didn't know what Jamie could be talking about. I didn't know if he was talking about mom or what.

"What is it Jamie? You sound serious about it."

"Do you remember when we were in court and it came out that I was sleeping with Shawna?

"Yeah….."

"Remember she was pregnant with Terrance's baby?"

"Yeah….." I didn't know where Jamie was going with this conversation. Was he going to tell me Shawna was dead or something?

"Well, it's actually my baby, Tonya."

My mouth dropped. I was instantly angry. That bitch. She had everyone believing that was Terrance's baby. She knew damn well it wasn't. That lying bitch. Then a smirk came over my face.

"So I have a niece or nephew?"

"A niece."

"How do you know it's yours?"

"I saw her for the first time two months ago. She has my green eyes. Her name is Morgan."

"Will I get to see her?"

"I don't know. Shawna and I are still working out the details with me seeing her, so I'm not sure about you."

"She can't keep you away from your daughter."

"No, she can't. But with everything she has been through. I don't want to pressure her."

10

I did forget I tried to kill her. Then I threatened to kill her again. She lost her husband too. Shawna has been through a lot. I felt some type of joy inside knowing that I had a niece. Neither Jamie nor I had any children, so I desperately wanted to see my niece. I doubt Shawna would want me anywhere near her. But all I ever wanted was a child of my own, and now I'm an Auntie. That also meant I was part of the family now. I had never been a part of anything but my own family. But with Jamie and Shawna having a baby together, it made me family too.

Jamie

Today was the day I picked up Tonya from the psychiatric hospital. It had been nine long months of treatment. She was finally coming home. Tonya didn't have a place to go, so I offered to let her stay with Dana and I until she got on her feet. Dana was against it, saying she should go live with mom. I was all my sister had. Mom refused to visit her in the psychiatric hospital. I didn't blame her. After a few visits, I got used to it.

Dana and I didn't argue much. I've never lived with anyone before except my mom. The experience was much different than I imagined. I still had a wall up. We didn't go out on dates much. I had a complex about public displays of affection. I didn't know how much longer that would last until he said something. Although I was in a relationship with this man, I still wasn't ready to fully "come out" with him. I had a daughter now which made the circumstances much different. I never envisioned it would be like this. I just didn't feel "right" being with a man and having a daughter. It made me feel like I "should" be with a woman. I didn't want my daughter growing up confused. Dana thought that I should just let Shawna be and not be involved in my daughter's life. I could never do that. Shawna let me see Morgan once. She was so beautiful. I could never deny her.

The reality hit that Terrance was dead when Shawna began working from home. Everything was so surreal. I attended the funeral, but I stood in the way back where no one could see me. Terrance had some extended family members that I didn't ever know about. Everyone found out that day that Terrance had a twin brother Terrell. Shawna was surprised as well as their son TJ. Terrell was identical to Terrance except he didn't have the same hardness about him. It appeared that he was more on the professional side of things. It looked like he could have been a lawyer or something. It was almost like seeing a ghost when Terrell appeared. My heart skipped a beat. I thought Terrance came back from the dead himself. I slid out of the funeral before anyone saw me. I had to pay my last respects.

Shawna and I were still cordial to one another despite the mishaps that had happened. I knew she would never agree to let Tonya see the baby. I don't blame her. She could hurt the baby out of spite. That would be the day I probably would try to kill my sister myself. I was still fighting an internal battle with myself about my sexuality. I'd been debating over the last few months to call Victor to see how he managed the confusion. I knew he was busy. The last time we spoke about two months ago, he wanted to move back home closer to his children in Virginia. I didn't blame him, I would miss my kids too. He could practice law anywhere. I didn't want to keep denying who I really was. The question was who am I? When do I stop running for myself?

14

Brian

I was sitting in my office reminiscing about childhood memories. Terrance and I were friends since we were about eight years old. Terrance was the only one that was nice to me. I watched him hustle and take care of his sisters after his mom's death. He took care of them and sent them to college. He paid for both of their tuition. I don't ever think he got a single thank you from Tamia or Talyah. It was fucked up how everybody turned their back on him, after all that he did. He didn't kill his baby brother. The streets did. Terrance was trying to look out for him by taking him under his wing. But his family didn't see it that way. Daron was a knucklehead trying to follow behind Terrance. If they should have been mad at anyone, it should have been Terrell. Terrell was the one that turned his back on his family. As soon as he turned 18, he left and never looked back. He left the burden of taking care of his family on Terrance. If everyone was so concerned about Daron, then Terrell should have stepped up. I never knew Terrell that well, he was the opposite of Terrance I heard. He wasn't as social, definitely a homebody. I always thought that maybe he wasn't right in the head.

I didn't fit in with a lot of the other kids in school, even though I wanted to. Terrance went out of his way to make sure I was good. I kept my head in the books and got good grades. I didn't need it like Terrance to survive, but I wanted to eat too. My mom didn't struggle with me, but we did our best. I didn't meet my father until I was 16 years old. Terrance never knew his father. We both had that in common. We were so much like each other, but so much different from each other. Terrance was street savvy. He had a mouthpiece, a good sales person. He could always talk a good game, no matter the circumstances. I watched him be reckless with his money. I enjoyed some of it too. My father came around sporadically. He paid for my college tuition, and we never spoke about it.

When Terrance and I turned 18, we kind of went our separate ways. I tried to hang with him back home, but I got so tied up with school. I also couldn't risk hanging out with him and getting in trouble. We stayed our distance from each other. We always partied when we saw one another. Terrance was coming up, and his name rang in the streets. I earned a lot of street cred just from being with him.

I remembered the day Terrance wanted to team up and open our own business.

"Yo Brian, I want to open up my own business."

"What kind of business?"

"I don't know. I want to wash this money. I want clean money. What kind of degree did you get?"

"Business with a minor in Finance."

"Man, what if we opened one of those bank firms?"

"Investment firm?"

"Yeah, one of those."

"You need a lot of money to start one of those."

"Like how much?"

"The startup cost alone will probably break you."

I underestimated how long Terrance's money was. I didn't know what kind of money he had. I threw a number out to see if he would bite.

"The startup cost alone is probably about $3 million. But we will get that back once we begin partnerships with other firms."

"Aight, I got that."

I was impressed.

"T, how much money do you have if you don't mind me asking?"

"Man, I don' know. I stopped counting around $10 million"

"Where is it?"

I knew he didn't house this money in a bank. They would have been all over him.
"I can't tell you all that right now. In due time man."

I didn't believe Terrance when he said he had $10 million. There was no way. It was possible. Terrance had been in the game since we were about 15. We were 24 now. Terrance was a spender, but he was also a saver. He owned a whole apartment building. His apartment was nice and decorated well. He was dating this woman named Sherrell at the time. She was too good for him. One of those good girls. She wanted him to get out the game. I think that is why he came to me asking to be clean. He wanted to marry her. He knew he had to do right by her before she left him. I guess she didn't want to wait any longer.

After that break-up Terrance was on a mission. Terrance had a lot of connections. That night we went to a warehouse. He had one of those bank safes with the wheel and everything. I'd never seen so much money in my life. I told Terrance we needed to count it. Back then I was much more loyal to Terrance. Terrance had a little over $17 million dollars. We both put in work. I put in most of the background work. He put up the money. I had the experience.

That night he met Shawna and I met Lisa we'd been celebrating. We had closed a major deal, and we were on our way. I peeped Lisa checking Terrance out long before he stepped to Shawna. But I was checking Lisa out. In my opinion, Lisa was much more attractive than Shawna. But you let Terrance tell it, Shawna was more attractive than Lisa.

Lisa stood about 5'6, light brown skin complexion, maybe about 140-150 pounds, short hair. She was about a shade darker than Shawna. That night Shawna didn't go home with Terrance, but I went home with Lisa. Lisa and I started dating. I was really feeling Lisa. A few weeks went by, Terrance never even contacted Shawna. I had listened to Lisa talk about it relentlessly.

We saw our ticket when Terrance had a meeting with a new investor and realized that Shawna was the one in charge. Terrance's whole mindset changed. He liked Shawna, but he wasn't over Sherrell. He made himself get over Sherrell. The rest was history.

Lisa

Although it had been six months since the passing of
Terrance, our wedding plans had been put on hold. I
was tired of waiting, I wanted to get married now.
Shawna and I hadn't talked since her daughter was
born. Yeah, I'm a fucked up friend. I didn't care
anymore, but I needed to play nice.

Shawna and I had been friends since junior high. I was
the popular one, she wasn't. I brought her into my
circle. Shawna came into her looks around high school.
She gained more attention than I did. Shawna had it all,
she was the beauty and brains. I was just pretty. I
barely made it through high school. Shawna tried to be
a good friend and encourage me to go to college. It
wasn't my thing. Truth was, I couldn't leave my mother
and my sister. I spent a lot of time taking care of them. I
had to work to help out around the house. I always
dated the guys that were thugs or flashy. I needed the
money, so I did what I needed to do to make sure I got
what I wanted. Shawna was respectable. She didn't get
down like that, but she never judged me for it either.

When Shawna went to college. I felt alone. When I
called her she always seemed too "busy." When she
finished college, she gave me a job at her firm. I was
grateful. I made great money, but felt like she could be
paying me more to be her assistant. She only paid me

$50,000 a year. I always felt like I played seconds to Shawna, no matter the circumstances.

The night I met Brian. I was checking out Terrance. I saw him first. Terrance was fine as hell, and just like I liked them, flashy and fine. I wanted him, but he had his eye on Shawna. Shawna being the dignified women she was decided she wasn't going home with Terrance that night. I wanted to though. But his sidekick Brian was so interested in me, I decided to show some interest. I didn't want the sidekick, I wanted the one that was in charge. Brian is a good man. I went home with him, I gave him some ass after seeing how he lived. We saw each other for a few weeks. Terrance would come over sporadically. I damned near lived with Brian as much as I was there. Terrance had a key to Brian's apartment. He always knocked before he came in.

"Brian here?"

"Nope."

"Damn, tell him to call me when he get in. I haven't been able to get in touch with him all day."

"Aight." He turned to leave.

"Wait."

"What's up, Lisa?"

"What's up with you and Shawna? Why haven't you called her?"

"Look, I'm not ready for nothing serious. Your girl cool and all. But I'm just trying to fuck something."

"Oh yeah?"

"Yeah."

"Well here is my number whenever you're trying to fuck something." I said seductively.

"You Brian girl. That's my best friend. I can't do that."

"We not serious like that. Call me."

Terrance didn't say anything, he just left. I wondered did I put myself out there too much. Would he tell Brian? I may have fucked up.

Brian came home about an hour later. I told him I had to leave to take care of my mother for a few hours. I would see him tomorrow. Truth was, I got the text from Terrance. I wanted to see what he was working with. But I wanted to get to him before Shawna did. I saw him when he slid his number to her before he left. If I could put it down good enough. I could make him forget all about Shawna.

"What's up?"

"Ain't shit."

"You trying to fuck or what?"

"You know what's up."

I got undressed. He bent me over the couch and just started fucking me. I came all over his dick. The dick was good. I knew I had to get more of it. I was ready for round two. He got a phone call right before he was ready to give me round two. I already knew who it was. Shawna and I had talked before so I knew she was going to call.

"Well, let's get one for the road."

We fucked one more time. Who knew that would be the last time.

"Look, you gotta go." He didn't even make eye contact.

I got up and put on my clothes. I was disappointed he kicked me to the curb for Shawna. I went to my mom's house and took a shower. I hoped he wasn't going to tell Brian. He has just as much to lose as I did. But I hoped I left a big enough impression on him for him to not even take Shawna seriously.

Later that night, I got a call from Shawna.

"Hey girl."

"Hey." I said flatly.

"Guess what?"

"What?"

"I had a date with that guy from the club tonight. He was so gentlemen like. I really like him Lisa."

"That's cool."

"I don't want to let this affect the company potentially partnering with them."

"Well don't do nothing with him until you have reviewed those numbers. If they look good, then go with it."

I was jealous of Shawna's date with Terrance. I felt like Terrance was just using her to get in. I guess I was wrong, because within six months, they got married, brought a house then had a baby. Terrance threatened me not to tell Shawna about what we did. I knew he was from the streets, so I didn't want him to follow through with his threats.

Fast forward almost a decade, I am still in love with idea of Brian. He is a good guy. He is part owner of this multi-million-dollar company, he has his own company, car everything. He is a great cook. He is the total package. His dick is even a nice size. There was nothing bad I could say about Brian other than he just wasn't for me. I wanted to marry him because I knew I would be taken care of for life, in spite of him wanting me to sign pre-nuptial papers. I desperately wanted to have his baby because at least if I had his child, I knew I had an attachment to him. He kept putting this wedding off. I feel like I've been wedding planning by myself. We would have to talk about this tonight when he got home.

Meanwhile, I was still Shawna's assistant at her firm. Shawna worked from home, so I had little contact with her except via e-mail. If she needed something at the office, I would scan it and e-mail it to her. She mostly kept her work at home. It made it harder to know what she was doing and what kind of numbers she was working with. I despised being Shawna's assistant. I wanted to be married, so I wouldn't have to work anymore. I wanted Shawna's life. Shawna's life was supposed to be my life.

Shawna

I couldn't believe at almost 35 years old, I was a widow. TJ was still grieving for his father. I didn't know how many other ways to tell him that his father wasn't coming back. Terrell had stopped by a few times. But that just made it harder on TJ, so I stopped him from coming. It was also becoming difficult for me to see Terrell's face. He meant well, but I couldn't handle it either. We have been communicating over the phone and e-mail. Terrell wanted to be there for us. I wanted to let him. I allowed Terrell to handle some affairs for me because there were something things going on with some accounts. After Mr. Johnson passed away, I knew it was just me and Jamie. I didn't want to alarm Jamie if I didn't have to, especially if nothing was going on. I wanted to trust Brian, but my gut was telling me not to. I'd been in communication with Terrell and e-mailed him documents to take to Brian. I needed him to check on those items for me.

My doctor suggested therapy. I didn't completely dismiss the thought of therapy. I was sure that I needed someone to talk to. I just wasn't ready. I shut everyone else out again except my mother. My mother moved in with me after Terrance passed away. Lisa hasn't visited me since Terrance passed away. She hasn't called other than it was work related. Some friend. I was upset that she hadn't reached out to me. I felt like I needed her more than ever.

Morgan was almost seven months old. I let Jamie visit once to see her. I wasn't sure how I felt about it all. I didn't know if I should allow him to be a part of her life or not. I didn't approve of his lifestyle, nor did I want Morgan exposed to it. But it was *his* child. I couldn't deny him that. I made a mental note to at least schedule every other week visitation with Jamie. There was no denying that she belonged to Jamie, from her green eyes, to her brown curly hair. She was definitely his. There was no reason for Jamie to miss anymore of Morgan's milestones.

Ever since they reopened Terrance's murder investigation. I've been on pins and needles. I didn't know anything about Terrance's lifestyle prior to us getting married other than he was just starting up his business. I wondered what other secrets he could be hiding. My mom interrupted my thoughts.

"Shawna, open up some blinds in here! You're living like a vampire," mom said.

I squinted my eyes because the sun was sensitive to my eyes.

"I'm not living like a vampire. I just prefer it to be dark."

"I'm not living like no vampire Shawna. We need light. These kids need light. Look how pale they have gotten."

My mom has always had a way of exaggerating. I don't know what I would do without her. She took Morgan out of the house. She played with TJ. She made sure TJ got to school. I haven't left the house since Terrance passed away. I knew it was time for me to get out of the house. I haven't even gotten rid of Terrance's things. I couldn't bring myself to. After everything that man has did, I still loved him. I just wanted him back.

My life had been a whirlwind. I knew things couldn't get any worse.

T

It was always hard being a twin and living in the shadows of Terrance. The hardest part was that we were identical. No one could ever tell us apart. People nicknamed me T first because my name was Terrell. But Terrance took that too. People ended up calling him T-Money instead. Terrance and I never really got along growing up. We only interacted because mom said we had to. We were complete opposites. Terrance was attracted to materialistic things, while I was attracted to learning things. I kept my head in the books. Terrance ran the streets. We couldn't be more different from one another.

I think our mother dying was the hardest thing any of us had to face. We were already fatherless, now we were motherless. Terrance stayed behind to make sure our brother and sisters were good. I felt bad for leaving. If I didn't, I would have spent another few years trying to get out of that hell hole. I left and never looked back. I gave props to Terrance for taking care of everyone, so they wouldn't go to foster care. He was a better man than me. Our baby brother Daron was killed years ago. I knew it wasn't Terrance's fault that Daron was killed. It just gave me more of a reason to stay away from him. Talyah and Tamia were more unforgiving. It was probably because they were closer in age with Daron.

Terrance's death came as a surprise. I was sure that Terrance would be dead long before now. I swear that man had luck on his side. Terrance had never been to jail and he made it to the age of 30. He was a real-life drug dealer turned Wall Street hustler. I was impressed with Terrance. He had his shit together. When he called me to redo his will, I was more than impressed. That man had more money than me, more assets than me and less liabilities than me. He knew his shit after all. Terrance seemed spooked when he called me. I knew it was serious. We hadn't talked in five or six years. I wasn't sure if karma had caught up to him, or he was paranoid. Whatever it was, he was desperate. I heard some rumor about Terrance before he passed. People were saying he was on the DL. I didn't know how true it was. I wanted that secret or rumor to die with Terrance.

I was trying to be there for Shawna. I could tell that it was difficult for Shawna to see me because I was identical to Terrance. There was no telling us apart. I wanted Shawna to know that I was there for us regardless the circumstances. I moved to Maryland to be closer to them. I could open up my business anywhere.

I had made a mental note to stop by the Terrance's company when I had a chance. Shawna wanted me to check on some things for her. She told me that I didn't need to speak to Brian, and she would make sure to tell him. I met Brian a few times when I was younger. He never fit in with Terrance. Terrance liked him, so he stuck around. All I knew is now that Brian is co-owner with Shawna, anything that he did had to go through her. That could probably be a pain in the ass. Shawna knew her shit as well. How she hooked up with a man like Terrance? I will never know.

I stopped by the office and was very much impressed by the company that Terrance and Shawna built. I walked up to the receptionist desk. This beautiful young lady greeted me. She looked spooked.

"How, um, how can I help you today?"

"Yes, I'm here to see Brian Tompkins."

"Can I tell him who's here to see him?"

"Yes, Terrell James."

"Thank You, you may have a seat."

I didn't feel the need to tell this young lady whom probably knew Terrance that I was his twin brother. After all it was none of her business. I was here on business that's it. I wanted to help my sister-in-law as much as possible.

Brian stepped out of his office, looking much different than I remembered. He looked like he made something of himself. One thing Terrance and I had in common was that both of us were very intuitive. Maybe it was a twin thing.

"Mr. James, what brings you here today?"

"Call me Terrell, and I'm just here checking on somethings for Shawna. Do you have a moment?"

"Sure."

We returned to his office. I sensed a nervous energy from him. Was he hiding something?

"It's been a long time since I've seen you Terrell, how are you holding up?"

"I'm well. Just trying to get some affairs in order for Shawna that's all."

"Well, how can I help you?"

I reached in my bag and pulled out some papers. I knew what I needed to know to ask the appropriate questions.

"Shawna wants to know about these four accounts. She doesn't understand where the money is going even with all the growth. It is her understanding that these should be the correct numbers for these accounts." I slid the papers in front of him. He skimmed over them and his confusion turned into concern.

"Terrell, I don't have time to look into these today. But I will most definitely look into them."

"Brian, I need an answer by the end of the day about this money. Do whatever you need to do, but don't keep me waiting."

Brian

Shawna was becoming a real pain in my ass. Every month she requested reports, all of them. Shawna definitely knew her shit, which was another reason I needed to get her away from the company. This was my company by default. Even in death, that son of a bitch made sure I didn't have the entire company. I thought it was fucked up. We talked about it so many times. I just knew he would leave me his share of the company. I guess you never really know a person despite what they say.

Terrell showed up to the company. I could tell Lisa was spooked but I already knew who it was when he showed up. I thought Terrell lived down south some where. I didn't understand what he was doing here. He began grilling me about four accounts that Shawna wanted to know about. Those were the same four accounts that I was storing money in an off-shore account. I tried to play cool about it but I told Terrell I would look into it. I could definitely tell that he was a lot more cutthroat than Terrance, and he knew his shit. I had to be careful with Terrell and Shawna.

I had to be on my shit when it came to Shawna. There was no more hiding money in our off-shore account. Lisa began nagging me more and more about walking down the aisle. I gave her a ring to shut her ass up. I did love her once upon a time. But I needed her more than I loved her.

I had so much information against Terrance. It was enough to put him away for life. I knew he wasn't responsible for Daron's death. He loved that boy to death. I went to the police to tell them that he was responsible and had intimate details. This was way before shit fell apart with him and I. This was around the time when we first opened the company. I wanted them to have a paper trail on Terrance, so when shit went south, it would be all him. None of it could be pinned back on me. I didn't know who wanted Terrance dead so bad. It could have been some folk back home. Terrance was living a double life, so maybe it came back to haunt him. They said that his side chick killed him. I believe it. That chick was crazy. I kept telling Terrance to leave her alone. But for five damn years, he strung that chick along. What did he think was going to happen with a woman like that?

I felt like Lisa and I would be the Terrance and Shawna. They just seemed to have it together. No one knew how much Lisa and I struggled. We struggled to have a baby. We damn near went broke trying in-vitro. Eventually we stopped. That was the reason I started storing money in an offshore account. Lisa and I brought a house together. It's actually my house she just lives in it. After Terrell left, Lisa popped in my office.

"Hey Brian, umm why do I feel like I've just seen a ghost."

"Oh, nah that's Terrance's twin brother."

"Shit are they identical?"

"Yeah."

"Damn, that's kind of creepy."

"Yea it is, but I already knew who he was. Is there anything else Lisa?" I was annoyed.

"Are you busy?"

"Nah, what's up?"

"I wanted you to look over these colors to see if you like them. I thought we could…"

I cut her off in mid-sentence.

"Look Lisa, I don't want to talk about no damn wedding planning right now." I was in a whole totally different mood since Terrell visited.

"If not know, then when?" I could tell she was irritated.

"I don't know Lisa!"

"You proposed to me almost a year ago and we aren't even close to walking down the aisle! Did you get me a ring to shut me up?"

"No, of course not!" I did, but I wasn't going to tell her that.

I didn't know how much longer I could put off this wedding planning. It wasn't like Lisa had many friends to begin with.

"Whatever Brian! We will talk about this later." I sensed the demanding tone and knew we would talk about it later.

I didn't know what to do about these accounts. I wondered how long I could put it off. I sat there for almost an hour looking at those reports. Then I sat them to the side. It was Friday, I wasn't going to stress. Shawna could wait.

I hadn't seen Terrell since we were kids. He seemed like he was anti-social, nothing like Terrance. The only way to tell Terrell from Terrance back then was their mouthpiece. Terrance was outspoken. Terrell was not. But he came in the office with confidence today. He almost reminded me of Terrance. But it was something about his personality that I definitely knew that it wasn't him. Besides he was dead anyway.

Lisa was becoming a pain in my ass, but I needed to be sure I actually wanted to marry Lisa before I walked down the aisle with her.

Tonya

We finally made it back to Jamie's house. I realized I'd never visited Jamie's home before. It was nice. It was beyond nice. It was decked out. I was in awe walking around his home. I walked into the kitchen, and saw his boyfriend cooking.

"Hey Tonya, it's finally nice to meet you." He stuck out his hand for me to shake it.

"Hi….." I paused. He was too bubbly for me.

"I wanted to make some lunch for you. I know you're probably tired of that hospital food."

"Yeah, actually I am!" I was excited.

"I guess we all have one thing in common." He shot a look at Jamie.

"What's that?"

"That is nothing to worry about Tonya." Jamie said interrupting Dana. "Let me show you to your room."

I saw Jamie give him the side eye.

"What was that all about Jamie?"

"Nothing."
"Tell me. He is probably going to tell me when you aren't around anyway."

He looked like he was thinking about it.

"You're right it should come from me."

I was concerned because I didn't know what Jamie was about to say.

"Dana also slept with Terrance too. It was before my situationship with Terrance, but during your relationship with Terrance."

I started getting sick to my stomach. Everyone under this fucking roof had slept with Terrance. I began thinking that Terrance wasn't that great guy I made him out to be.

"Damn. It's ok. Nothing I can do about it now. He's dead."

I made up my mind I would be single for the rest of my life. Terrance fucked me up so bad. I was just trying to pick up the broken pieces of my life. I've spent the last two years of my life obsessing over Terrance. Now he's dead. He left his wife everything. I'm a nobody. I couldn't figure out for the life of me how I got myself into that fucked up situation.

"Tonya, there is something else that I need to talk to you about."

I didn't know what it was that Jamie could possibly tell me now that wouldn't make my world even more fucked up than it already is.

"Shawna….." he paused.

"Ugh, what about her? Matter of fact I don't even want to hear her name anymore."

"I know, I know. Ummm, she will be a permanent part of our lives moving forward."

"What do you mean? She has her own life, with her own kids."

"Well…..remember we have a daughter together."

"Yea, yea I know, I know."

"This is serious Tonya, I need to know that you aren't going to hurt her."

"Jamie! I can't even imagine that you would even think something like that!"

"I had to ask. It's not that I don't trust you."

"It's that you don't trust me." I mumbled.

I felt like Shawna had ruined my life. Wait, no my therapist said that I had to take accountability for my own actions. I ruined my own life. Shawna was just a part of the process. I made each decision to move forward with Terrance knowing his situation. I finally wanted Shawna out of my life. Now there is no chance of that ever happening. I had to make the best out of a bad situation. This wasn't a bad situation, just an annoying one.

Lisa

I was sitting at my desk looking through floral arrangements for the wedding, when a voice that was familiar to me gave me chills. I looked up and it was a man that looked like Terrance, sounded like Terrance. But there was no way it could be Terrance. It sent chills up my spine just to even speak to him. When he looked at me, I felt like he could see into my soul. I waited from Brian to come out of his office. He looked annoyed, but not fearful as I was when he saw this Terrance look-a-like. When Brian emerged from his office again. I pounced on the opportunity to talk to him about wedding planning. I didn't want to feel like I was planning this wedding all by myself.

Brian always seemed annoyed with me. After he told me that was Terrance's twin brother Terrell. I felt more relieved. I knew there could be no way it could have been Terrance. Brian told me he would talk to me later about the wedding planning. I was beginning to think this wedding may never happen. If Terrance and I were together, I would have never had to worry about him proposing. He would have just done it. It was silly of me to think this way. I didn't know if I was doing all of this wedding planning to make myself feel better or just to kill time. I didn't know if I still had bridesmaids or a maid of honor. I hadn't talk to Shawna over the phone since Morgan was born. I visited a few times in the beginning because they are my godchildren. Nothing more than that. Am I horrible friend?

Jealousy overwhelmed me. Shawna had nothing. Her husband was dead, raising two children by herself, no support except from her mother. But I was still jealous. I had to really re-evaluate why I was still jealous of Shawna. Was it because I thought that she was more successful than I was? Even after all that she has been through, she is still standing. She hasn't let any of this break her. She should be broken. She should have lost everything, and she didn't. Maybe I should visit. I didn't have a reason to visit, I would feel like I'm visiting out of guilt. What kind of friend am I?

I didn't understand why Brian was stringing me along. I've never given him a reason to doubt us. I've never cheated on him. There was this one time. But I feel like it didn't count because we weren't official. As soon as I saw that he moved on, that was over. He couldn't possibly know, could he? Could that be the reason he hasn't walked down the aisle with me yet? I convinced myself that it couldn't be true. He would have left me a long time ago if that were true. Maybe he just has cold feet. I needed to hold on to something with Brian. He was the only thing that was stable in my life. I would have to start all over if we broke up. The thought of that made me nervous. I feared that more than him finding out about Terrance. I had to figure out a way to talk to Brian without upsetting him. It has been more difficult since Terrance has died. I have to figure out a way.

Shawna

When I sent Terrell to find out what was going on with those four accounts, I didn't know what information he would come back with. I thought that I may have been reading too much into the accounts. I wanted to make sure what I was seeing was correct. When Terrell comes back from his meeting with Brian, I will know 100 percent if Brian has been stealing money from the company. If all of this is true, then Mr. Johnson *was* wrong. It was Brian all along. It would have made more sense for Brian to be behind all of it. There was no way Terrance could pull it off by himself. I don't discredit Terrance for any hard work he has put in, but to pull something like this off takes major skills. It takes someone that knows the ins and outs, that knows how to make it look good on paper to the untrained eye. I haven't been a part of the business for a while, so reconciling these accounts wasn't as easy as I remembered. I heard a knock at the door. I looked through the peephole and it was Terrell. It was getting harder and harder to see him.

"Hey Terrell." We embraced.

"Hey Shawna."

"What did you find out?"

"Nothing yet. I gave him until 5:00 p.m. today."

"Ok. I was looking at these accounts again today. It would take someone that has been in the business and knows the business to pull of something like this. I don't discredit Terrance, but Terrance wouldn't have been able to pull this off."

"What do you mean?"

"I mean Terrance may have been smart and business savvy, but there is just no way he could have pulled this off without having some type of help."

"Hmph."

"Daddddddddddyyyyyyy." TJ hopped up on Terrell.

"No TJ that isn't daddy. That's Uncle Terrell. Remember I told you the story about daddy."

"Yes," his face saddened. I'm sorry Uncle Terrell.

"It's ok little man. Everybody used to get us confused growing up. Nobody and I mean nobody could tell the difference." He winked.

Terrell looked at me and smiled. He even smiled like Terrance.

"TJ, can I talk to Uncle Terrell for a moment? Do you mind going upstairs?"

46

"Sure! I'm gonna go and watch some cartoons."

I waited for TJ to be out of earshot and then spoke to Terrell.

"What did you find out?"

"Brian did seem startled by my presence, but even more nervous when I asked him about these accounts. He acted as if he wanted to write it off as nothing until I made it about something."

"I'm telling you Terrell, it's not adding up. Nothing is. These reports, these accounts, they don't make sense."

"I gave him until 5 p.m. today, so we will see what he says."

I checked my time and Terrell checked his too.

Something was fishy about Brian but I couldn't put my finger on it.

Brian

Time was winding down to reconcile these accounts. I knew Shawna would be calling soon if I didn't have an answer for her. I was stuck in a bind. I couldn't put this off on Terrance anymore because he was gone. I couldn't talk to Lisa because she doesn't know about it either. I called the only man that I felt like owed me everything.

"Hi Dad."

"Hey, hey Brian. What's going on? How are you doing?"

"Dad, I got a bit of a problem. I don't know if you can help me or not."

"I can do my best."

"What I am about to ask you can't be shared with anyone, and you can't tell anyone about what I'm about to ask you."

"Brian, you know I can keep a secret."

I got up to close my door, because I didn't want anyone listening to my conversation.

"I'm in trouble, big trouble. I need some help. It's these accounts and I don't know how to reconcile them without raising any red flags."

"What do you mean?"
I took a deep breath.

"I've been taking money out of these accounts and putting it in off-shore accounts. These folks are dead and their family doesn't even know there is money still being returned in the account. My boss started looking into these accounts and I don't know how to fix it."

The silence over the phone was eerie. I felt like a weight had been lifted off my shoulders when I told him that. I have never told anyone else that information.

"Dad, are you there?"

"Yes, I'm here. I'm just thinking. I know a guy. I'm not sure if he is into this kind of stuff anymore, but it is definitely worth a shot. When do you need this information by?"

"Today by 5 p.m."

"Brian, why didn't you call earlier. This might be tough. But I'll call you right back."

"Thanks Dad."

I always used my father whenever I needed him. We never had a close relationship. He mainly tried to buy me with money because he wasn't there for the majority of my childhood. I was ok with that. My mom made sure we didn't struggle that hard. My father had connections, I was just praying that he would come through with them.

T

I left Shawna's house and grabbed a late lunch while I waited on Brian to get this shit straight. If Shawna had a hunch, I believed her. From what I knew about Shawna she was always on her shit. I could definitely tell that by the way she projected herself. I arrived at this restaurant on the other side of town. I wasn't really familiar with it, but I felt like I couldn't go wrong. I was seated by a waitress that kept grinning at me from ear to ear. I wasn't here to talk to anyone.

"Hi, my name is Amber. I will be your server. Can I get you something to drink?"

"Yes, a rum and coke. Thank you."

"I will be right back."

The waitress returned with my drink. It was hard choosing something to eat, everything looked so appetizing.

"What do you recommend?"

"We have a special today. It's our homemade spaghetti with meatballs. The customers love it."

"You know what, that is my favorite. I will have that."

I took out my phone to check a few e-mails, and check on my lovely little fling back home. I hadn't gotten in touch with too many people since I left. Since I had some down time it was the perfect time until I was interrupted again.

"Excuse me."

"Yes." I looked up in confusion.

"Are you….are you….?"

"Am I what?" I was confused. I didn't know this woman. But obviously she knew me or did she know Terrance? I continue to forget that I am in his city.

"I'm sorry. I swear they say everyone has a twin. You look exactly like this man I used to date named Terrance."

I already knew where this conversation was going. I knew Terrance didn't tell many people about me because the family disowned him. I felt like I needed to introduce myself.

"My name is Terrell. I am Terrance's twin brother."

"I'm so so sorry! I feel so embarrassed."

"It's ok what's your name?"

"My name is Latonya. Latonya Billiard."

"Why don't you have a seat Latonya?" It's nice getting to know Terrance's old friends."

It felt awkward meeting with this woman. But she was obviously in awe. She hardly said anything when she sat down. I wanted to let her lead and talk if she wanted to.

"Um, so um do you live here?"

"Yes, I do now. I'm here helping Shawna out with some business things."

"Oh… her… I mean, how is she doing?"

I sensed some resentment from this Latonya woman. She must be a mistress. She said her and Terrance used to date.

"She is managing. Tell me how you knew Terrance." I deflected

"It's not important now. Maybe I should go."

I sensed her becoming uncomfortable so I let her go.

"It was nice to meet you Tonya."

When she looked back, she didn't speak. She just looked in complete shock. This was going to be interesting. Who else of Terrance's friends would I "run" into. I made a mental note to ask Shawna about her.

Tonya

After being bombarded with all the information that Jamie gave me a few days ago. I felt like I couldn't breathe, almost like I was having an anxiety attack. It was just too much for me to take in. His boyfriend was cool and all. He just seemed like he was smothering me. I couldn't deal. I appreciated everything that Jamie was doing for me. I knew I needed my own place really soon. The last year of my life had been pure hell. I knew I needed the support. I just didn't want to deal with all of this extra stuff now. I been out most of the day. I went shopping, got a pedicure and manicure now I was looking for somewhere to go and eat. I loved Italian food. You could never go wrong with Italian food. It was the restaurant over on the other side of town. It was a cute little spot. They had my favorite lasagna. I decided to treat myself. It wasn't like I had any friends. I waited to be seated. The hostess greeted me and took me to a little booth. I had my taste buds set on lasagna but everything else looked so good too. Maybe even the chicken parmesan. I looked up to see where my waitress was and I saw him. I thought I had seen a ghost. He looked like him, his mannerisms were like him. There was no way that could be *him.* Everything in me screamed not to go to the table. I had to. They say everyone has a twin and I believed it, because either my mind was playing tricks on me or it was Terrance's twin.

I was so nervous that I was stuttering over my words. I didn't know what to say. When he confirmed that he was Terrance's twin Terrell, it calmed my nerves a little. He invited me to sit down with him. I didn't want to because I was nervous. He began questioning how I knew Terrance. I didn't feel was important to bring up the details. I just told him I was just a friend. But something seemed off about him. I couldn't put my finger on it. He acted and spoke too much like Terrance. I shrugged it off because he was his twin. I never met a twin before, so maybe they had some sort of connection. Aren't they supposed to be alike?

The whole situation had played with my mind. I didn't even have an appetite afterwards. I just wanted to take my food to go. Now I knew he lived in the area. I just hoped that I wouldn't run into him anymore. I don't think my heart could take it. I felt like maybe the Gods were giving me a second chance. Maybe I wasn't supposed to be with Terrance, maybe it was supposed to be Terrell. Maybe God had mixed it up somehow. I had to think rationally. There was no way it was coincidence that I met his brother today at this restaurant. I felt like I needed to meet him again. Why didn't I think to get his number? I was so shaken up by the thought that it might be Terrance, that I couldn't think beyond that. If it was meant to be, we will run into each other again. I hoped we did.

On my way back home, I decided to take the long way home. I had so much on my mind. I wanted to relocate.

I wanted to runaway from it all, Shawna, Jamie, the past. Everything had been so traumatizing for me, and then people wonder why I'm crazy.

T

I finally got a phone call from Brian asking me to come by the office. It was after 5, but I would let him slide if things checked out. It was something off about the way Brian acted. I needed to see in person if he was as anxious as I thought he was. I got a to-go box and headed to his office. I was beginning to feel like I was doing Shawna's dirty work. Shawna told me that Terrance was stealing money from the company. Terrance is pretty street smart, but for him to embezzle money, I would never think so unless he had some help. Terrance hated a thief, so if he was one that would be different.

As I got to the building. I began to feel uneasy about this conversation that was about to happen. Something just didn't feel right. Everything in me was screaming to return in the morning when there were people in the office. I ignored my intuition and went anyway. I stepped off the elevator and Brian greeted me.

"How are you doing Terrell? I'm sorry about calling you after the deadline. I needed to wrap up some last-minute things."

"It's alright. I'm just glad that you could make the deadline." I sensed something off about Brian.

58

We made it back to his office, in which he handed me what looked like 10-sheets of paper.

"These are the numbers that you've requested, or should I say Shawna requested."

I ignored that part.

"Thank you Brian. I'll look over them later tonight, and get back with you."

I turned to walk away out of the office before Brian stopped me.

"Why are you doing Shawna's dirty work?"

"What do you mean?"

"I mean, Shawna sends you down here to look into some old accounts that aren't even on our radar, because she suspects something?"

"I'm just trying to help my sister-in-law out. She is going through a lot. If this makes it easier for her. I am more than willing to help her."

"Look Terrell, I know we have never been on the same page. But I need to remind you this is MY business. I don't care whose name is on the paperwork. Terrance and I built this company from the ground up. I won't have you or Shawna come in trying to take it from me."

"Is that a threat, Brian?" I smirked.

"No, it's not a threat, Terrell. I just wanted to let you know that I feel passionate about this company, and I will do whatever I need to do to keep it."

It was something sinister about the way he said that last statement. I couldn't let Brian get under my skin. I understood he was a little rattled about everything that was happening.

"No need for innuendos, I get the point Brian."

I hauled ass out of his office. Brian had something sinister about him going on. I couldn't put my finger on it. I was going to figure it out. I called Shawna while I was in the parking deck.

"Hey Shawna, I just stopped by Brian's office. I got the paperwork that you were looking for.

"Great, you can stop by if you'd like. I just made dinner for the kids. I need to see those numbers."

"Will do."

I felt good about helping Shawna. I just didn't know how much longer it would last. On the way to Shawna's I got a phone call from an unknown number.

"Hello. Hello. Hello."

No one said anything so I hung up. I hated
telemarketers.

Lisa

It was well after 6 when Brian made it home. I began to get a little worried because I hadn't heard from him. I knew tonight wasn't a good time to talk to him. He looked like he was pissed when he walked through the door.

"Hey babe."

"Hey," he said flatly.

"What's wrong?"

"Fuckin' Terrell! He slammed his hand down on the counter.

"Calm down! What about him?"

"He thinks that he can come up in MY company, and dictate what he needs. He doesn't know who he is messing with?"

"Wait, I thought Shawna needed whatever it was that Terrell sent him for."

"Yea…. she did." He had a look on his face like he was up to something.

"Why do you look like that?"

62

I have an idea. But you gotta stay with me on it.

"What is it?" I was curious because I rarely saw that look on his face.

"I need to get close to Shawna. Make her trust me."

"Well, how do you propose you do that? She don't even like you or talk to you." Whatever Brian was up to it was pretty sinister.

"No, I mean really get close to her. I'm going to have to play the comforting friend that is going to be there for her. As long as Terrell is there, he will be her right-hand person and not me. Even if I got to sleep with her, I'm willing to do whatever I need to do to keep my company."

"Do what! I think the hell not! Brian you have lost your damn mind if you think that I would let you go that far with Shawna!"

"What difference does it make Lisa? It's no different than when you were fucking Terrance while we were dating."

I felt like someone came and took the air out of the room. He caught me off guard. I didn't know what to say. My mouth was dry. I couldn't even get the words out. All these years I thought he didn't know.

"Yeah, I'm sure you thought I didn't know. I've always known Lisa. I was so love struck over you, I wanted to look past it. I hated Terrance, and you were jealous of Shawna. But I never knew why. It wasn't until Terrance told me a while back. I knew back then that you were probably willing to do anything I asked you to do, because you couldn't have Terrance.

"Fuck you Brian." I said quietly.

"Fuck me!" He pointed to himself.

"Fuck me! After everything I've done for you. I stayed with you even knowing that you fucked my best friend. But fuck me!" He laughed.

I began to tear up because I didn't realize how much it hurt to know that he was using me. It hurt even more to now know why he continue to postpone the wedding. He never had any intentions on marrying me.

"Brian, you're an asshole."

"I'm an asshole? You used me just like I used you. You were looking for security, I gave it to you. I just don't understand what the problem really is?"

"The problem is that you had no intention on marrying me, or having children. You keep leading me on thinking that we are going to get married!"

64

"Lisa, I did have intentions on marrying you. I even had intentions on having kids with you. But when I realized that you fucked my best friend early on, there was no coming back from that. What else was were you willing to do?"

"That was before you!" I lied.

"Before me? You sure?"

"I'm positive! We hadn't even hooked up yet. We were still just talking over the phone."

I had to make this shit right somehow. Make him somehow question Terrance. It wasn't like he was alive to defend himself now.

"Either way Lisa, whether it was before or after. You still fucked him. You wanted him before Shawna got to him. When he picked Shawna over you, that's when you decided to give me some play. I was always playing seconds to Terrance."

I had to make him believe that it wasn't the way he made it seem. But in truth, it was the way he made it seem. I did want Terrance. I was jealous of Shawna. Now that I'm fully vested in Brian he is just going throw in the towel and do what the fuck he wants to do?

There was no way he was about to leave me high and dry.

Brian

My father had come through. I didn't think he would but he did. Everything looked good. I only had a few minutes before Terrell showed up to look over everything. Terrell was on time and there to collect the paperwork. I wanted to challenge Terrell because I knew Shawna suspected something, but more importantly I wanted to see if Terrell would budge. There was something different about Terrell when I saw him earlier. He appeared to less confident this evening than when he walked in this morning. It was probably because him and I were the only ones in the office. I wasn't going to hurt Terrell, but definitely make him reconsider the fact that he even asked me for these documents in the first place. It was my company. Shawna just owns it. I deserve as much of it as anyone else. It wasn't fair that Terrance left Shawna everything. It just wasn't fair. After Terrell left, I took a deep breathe, opened my drawer where I keep my Vodka and took a drink right from the bottle. I just hoped that it would fly over with Shawna. I'd sat at the office way too long. It was time for me to go home. I knew Lisa would be calling soon if I didn't.

When I walked through the door I could already sense her attitude. I really didn't want to talk. I wasn't in a talking mood. But she had been getting on my damn nerves about this wedding planning shit. While at my office, I had conjured up a plan to get close to Shawna.

I knew that Lisa wouldn't go for it. But I was willing to do anything to keep my company. When I revealed that I knew she had slept with Terrance, she looked like she sprouted three heads. I knew she didn't think I knew. I didn't find out until a few years after Lisa and had already been in a relationship. I'd planned on marrying Lisa a long time ago, about two years after Terrance married Shawna. But a few years ago, when Terrance began cheating on Shawna, and he was drunk one night, he told me about him fucking Lisa. I didn't want to believe him, but I knew it could have been possible. As much as I tried to move forward and get it out of my mind I knew I couldn't trust her. At that point, I couldn't trust my best friend or my girlfriend. I had no one. It had all made sense of why Lisa was so jealous of Shawna. She felt like it should have been her instead of Shawna. Lisa felt like Terrance should have married her. I was a good guy. I had my share of infidelities, but that was only after I found out about her and Terrance.

We tried to have a baby in the beginning. When she did get pregnant. She lost the babies not once but twice. But ever since Terrance told me that they fucked, I started messing with someone else.
After she miscarried the second time, the other chick got pregnant again. So, she wanted to try invitro. We did. But they were all blanks. I told the doc not to tell Lisa, hell it wasn't her business anyway.

Naomi was, I guess you can call her the other woman. I had two children with her 5 and 3. Naomi lived in

68

California. I would go and see my children twice a month on the weekends. I paid all of her bills, sent her money whenever she needed, purchased her brand-new Escalade truck. Whatever Naomi needed I did for her. After all, she had my two children. She begged me to leave Lisa. But it was a part of me that couldn't part ways with her and I didn't want to lose my company. I know I used to scold Terrance for doing the same thing I'm doing. Hell, I'm not married to either one of them. It was easy to live this kind of a double life because they were so far apart from one another that I wouldn't have to worry about it.

I met Naomi about 8 years ago. I fell in love with her at business conference that Terrance and I went to in California. She was the most beautiful woman I'd ever seen. But when she spoke, my dick got hard and she wasn't even talking directly to me. I knew I had to have her. I was going back too far down memory lane. She had two of my babies, and the rest was history. We spoke about being together, but she didn't want to move. I didn't want to move. We just made shit work to fit our lifestyle. It was easy to get away from Lisa. She knew I owned a multi-million-dollar firm so I always had business meetings to go to. Lisa just didn't have the drive, the motivation to do anything else. She wasn't a go getter like Shawna. Although I despised Shawna, I admired her ambition, her drive. Lisa was just content. I needed someone to match me. Maybe one day Naomi and I would be together. She was a CFO for some big investment firm over in Cali. She lived a luxurious lifestyle that I was just trying to maintain. She became another reason I started embezzling money.

Shawna

I heard a knock on the door. I figured it had to be Terrell. I had been on edge all day waiting for him. But I didn't want to call in case he didn't come through. When I opened the door, I breathed a sigh of relief.

"Hey Shawna."

"Hey."

For some reason he smelled different. Why was I noticing that he smelled different?

"Here are the papers. I am not sure exactly what you're looking for. But all of the numbers looked good to me."

"I'll be the judge of that." As I snatched the papers from his hand.

There was something different about Terrell. Was I missing Terrance? Terrell stood there a little longer that I expected just staring at me.

"What!?

"Nothing, did you still need me to stay?"

"Uh, yeah, I guess you can stay. I cooked dinner tonight, so if you want some it's in the fridge."

"Nah, I'm ok. I had an early dinner."

I was distracted from looking over the paperwork he had given me. The numbers looked good, but these accounts did not. They looked too familiar to me but I couldn't put my finger on it where they were from. When I looked up, there he was staring at me again.

"What!?" I was annoyed now.

"Nothing, I'm sorry."

"What is it, Terrell?"

"Nothing Shawna, I should go."

I knew what it was. But I wasn't going to address it nor was he. Terrell had been stopping by so much it was difficult for me to not see Terrance in him. His mannerisms were much different, he spoke different, he even dressed different. That face, was still Terrance's face. He even had his line up the same as Terrance's. I didn't want to admit that I had an attraction to him. It was much different from an attraction I had to Terrance. Terrell had his shit together. He was smart, went to college, owned his own law firm. This was the kind of guy I was supposed to marry. What if somehow God had it mixed up? What if Terrell, was the one I was supposed to marry?

72

"You can stay. I'm sorry Terrell. I've just been in my feelings since I talked to the detectives today."
"Oh, you spoke with them again?"

"Yeah, he called. He said they were still investigating and were continuing to piece together this case. The way it was looking that Tonya didn't kill my husband."

"Tonya? Oh, Tonya! You mean the side chick?"

I cut my eye at him.

"I'm sorry that was so insensitive of me."

"It's ok. That's what she was. I wanted so bad for it to be her. I just wondered who else had it out for my husband that would have wanted him dead?"

"Shawna, I can tell you just being in this city for a little while. Terrance has definitely made himself quite a few friends and just as many enemies. There was a lot I didn't know about my brother. His old lifestyle could have easily came back to haunt him."

"I didn't know much about his old lifestyle. Do you? I know he said you left when y'all turned 18. But what was he doing before then? How did he get into this business?"

Terrell hesitated as if he didn't want to tell me. What harm could it do now? He was dead.

"That's not my story to tell, Shawna."

"Whose is it then? He isn't here to tell me. I'm just tired of everyone keeping secrets from me."

"Sit down. I'll tell you. I'm only telling you this because it can't come from him."

"Ok."

Terrell smelled so good. I got horny just at the thought of being next to him. I hadn't had sex in eight months. My toys just weren't cutting it anymore. I wanted him and I wanted him bad.

"Terrance was one of the biggest drug dealers to run the State of Maryland."

My mouth dropped wide open.

"I don't know if I would call him a kingpin or not. Terrance had a lot of money. He worked his way up and became the connect. He was no longer a small drug dealer making small money. He ran the whole thing."

"Stop it Terrell, you're lying!" I felt sick to my stomach.

"I'm not lying Shawna. Terrance money was very long, so long that it allowed him to open up his own investment firm to wash his money."

"My company," I said in a whisper.

"One of the main reasons that our sisters stopped talking to him because they felt like he was responsible for our youngest brother Daron's death. Terrance wanted to go to college like me and become something of himself. But the streets swallowed him whole. Instead of Daron going to work for some other drug dealer he started working for Terrance. Terrance thought if he could keep him close to him, he could keep him safe. When one of Terrance's houses got robbed, they killed Daron. My sisters blamed Terrance.

Terrell looked off as if he was staring into space.

"That is horrible. That wasn't his fault!"

"It wasn't. He was trying to help him. Terrance paid for me, Tamia and Talyah's college tuition. No financial aid or anything. He never even got a single thank you from his sisters or me.

"That's messed up."

"Yea it is." His voice drifted off. But that is his story. The short version."

"Wow! I guess there was a lot about Terrance that I didn't know about."

It made me wonder if that is why Terrance wanted to be so in control of my company. He wanted to wash his money. I know it was a thought that was far-fetched. But I couldn't help but to think of that was the case.

"Shawna, I gotta go. Let me know what you find."

"Will do!"

Jamie

I noticed that Tonya had been in her room the last few days. I just hoped that she was taking her medications like she should. Dana and I were a little rocky lately. Shawna had called a little over a week ago saying that she wanted to set up visitation for Morgan. I was more than excited to see my daughter. But Dana not so much. I was starting to believe that he was a bit jealous of Morgan. She was just a baby. Each day there was a new argument or snide remark.

"Hey babe." Dana said.

"Oh, you're talking to me now?"

"Yeah." He rolled his eyes. "Have you talked to Shawna again?"

"Not yet. I told her I would give her a call once I knew my schedule a little better."

"I don't understand why you need to have a relationship with *her* anyway."

"I don't even have any feelings for Shawna. I told you that I love you and only you. Why is it so hard for you to believe that?"

"Oh my God, I'm not even talking about HER. I'm talking about *her.*"

"My daughter?"

"Yes, *her.*"

"Look Dana, she is my daughter. Morgan came at a point in my life where things weren't cut and dry. Now that she is here, I want to have a relationship with her. Shawna is giving me that chance, and I want that chance to be a father to her. I don't get why you're jealous, or what you have against her."

"I don't have anything against her. I just feel like you're forcing a relationship with a little girl that might not even be yours. How do you know Shawna wasn't sleeping with anyone else? She *was* married. How do you know it isn't her husband's?"

Dana was really working my nerves. I had the same questions several months ago until I saw Morgan. She had my hazel eyes, with my curly brown hair. She looked nothing like Terrance. One thing I wasn't going to do was keep doing this dance with Dana over Morgan. I was seeing my daughter one way or another.

"Look Dana, I know it's hard to believe but she is mine. If you can't handle me having a relationship with my daughter, then I don't know what to tell you. She will be here every other weekend. I will be in her life."

78

"Are you choosing me over her?"

"There is no choosing you over her. What are you talking about? She is my daughter!"

"Choose Jamie. It's me or her."

"What?" I was confused.

"Me or Morgan."

"Dana, I'm not following. You want me to choose between you or my daughter?"

"Yes." He stood there with his arms crossed, tapping his foot.

"You're being unreasonable."

"Me or her, Jamie?"

I didn't want to have to make this decision. For the first time in my life I was a father. I thought that Dana would be more understanding than this.

"Dana, if this is what it comes down to. You know deep down what my choice is."

"I'll pack my things then."

I didn't want Dana to leave. But I wasn't going to abandon a relationship with my daughter.

"Dana, you can't be serious?"

"I'm very serious. I'm not ready to be a parent. As a matter of fact, I don't want children at all."

"Damn it Dana, if that was the case then why make me choose instead of just saying you don't want kids. You already sound insensitive as is. I guess you didn't want to make yourself sound like the asshole you are."

"Fuck you Jamie! You're so damn gullible!"

"Get the hell out of my house Dana!"

Dana had to be out of his damned mind if he thought that I was going to put him before my daughter. Instead of revealing he was just an asshole and didn't want children, he made it seem like I had to make a choice when really he needed to make a choice. Another one bites the dust.

Tonya

.

I had been so shaken up ever since I'd seen Terrell. I couldn't stop thinking about him. There was something about his mannerisms that were downright creepy. Even to the way he spoke reminded me of Terrance. Every twin has something different about them that someone can point out. I even noticed he was eating Terrance's favorite food. That was too much of a coincidence for me. I knew I had to see him again. I didn't want to become obsessed with him, just for my own peace of mind.

I woke up to Dana and Jamie arguing. It seemed like it was reoccurring thing now. They were always arguing over Jamie's daughter. I could see how Dana was upset. But his daughter was conceived before they were in relationship. Shawna had reached out to him to visit Morgan and establish visitation with him. I was actually surprised. I often wondered if Morgan was his. I didn't want Jamie to get his hopes us and this baby looked nothing like him. She would have nothing to gain by telling Jamie it's his baby though. I walked downstairs to see Jamie sitting on the couch with his hands coupling his face as if he was crying.

"Jamie."

"Yes," his voice crackled."

"Are you ok?"

"No, Tonya! I'm not ok. I wish I was ok."

"Did Dana leave?"

"Yeah…. we broke up!" Now he was sobbing.

"Oh, my goodness! Why?"

"He was trying to make me choose between him and Morgan!"

"What?"

"Yeah, he said that I had to make a choice, and of course I chose my daughter."

"You are right to choose your family over him. If he can't understand that, then it's his loss."

"Then he goes on to tell me that he never wanted children. This was never about me and Morgan in the first place. This was about him feeling left out."

"Oh wow! That is a tough pill to swallow, Jamie. Well, think of the bright side. Morgan didn't need that negativity around her anyway. This is a good thing."

"Maybe you're right, Tonya."

"Let's get some breakfast."

There was something I wanted to talk to Jamie about. I didn't want him thinking I was crazy again. He was the only one I could talk to. On our ride to grab breakfast, I broke the silence.

"Did you tell Shawna I was home?"

"No.....I didn't."

"Why not?"

"I will."

"You're not worried about me?"

"Should I be, Tonya?"

"No, you shouldn't. But I'm sure Shawna wouldn't agree."

I knew Shawna would have a difficult time with Morgan visiting him at his home especially if I'm there. Shawna had every right not to trust me. But this was Jamie's child "supposedly." If this was Jamie's daughter, I would never hurt my niece. Now if it was Terrance's daughter, Shawna might not see her again. I quickly dismissed those thoughts. I wasn't that person anymore.

"You've changed. I can see that. Besides….you wouldn't hurt Morgan anyway. She's your niece. No matter how much you hate Shawna, you love me."

"You're right. Just for the record I wouldn't hurt a child. You know I've always wanted a child myself."

"I know."

We changed topics. I didn't know how to bring it up without Jamie thinking I was "crazy" again.

"Jamie, I really need to talk to you about something but I don't want you to think I'm crazy."

Jamie's phone rang in the middle of what I was trying to discuss with him. We both got out of the car and waited. I'd never been to this breakfast spot before. I turned to scan the people and parking lot, and there he was again. At least I thought it was him. It was Terrell. He was walking in towards us. I had to see him. I had to hear his voice again. Something was off about him, and I needed to know if I was just being paranoid or it was just his brother.

"Hey!" I ran up to him.

"Hi," he looked confused.

"Remember me?"

"Uhhh… yeah. You're uhhhh…."

"Tonya. Remember I saw you last week at the Italian restaurant?"

"Oh yeah! Yeah, I remember."

Something was definitely off about Terrell today. This was not the same man that I met at the restaurant last week. Now I feel like I'm really tripping.

"How have you been?"

"Good, and yourself?"

"Pretty good, just maintaining."

The conversation was awkward and distant. When I saw him last week, his conversation made me feel comfortable, like I'd known him for awhile. Jamie walked up.

"Hey man, you must be Terrell?"

"Yeah…."

"I'm Jamie, I was a friend of Terrance."

"Ahhh ok, well it's nice to meet you. I'll catch you later."

He left quickly. I didn't know what to think of that moment. But now I really felt like I needed to talk to Jamie.

"That was interesting." Jamie said.

"Yeah.. it was."

"What is it that you wanted to talk to me about?"

We were now being seated. I knew what I wanted. Anything with pancakes and Jamie liked anything with waffles.

"Yeah… I don't know how to talk to you about this without sounding "crazy."

"Spit it out Tonya. I've seen it all with you. I don't think anything can surprise me anymore."

"Well, I'm just afraid that you will dismiss my feelings."

"Spit it out."

"Fine! Remember last week when I told you I wanted to go to the mall?"

"Yeah."

"On the way back, I decided to stop for something to eat. Guess who I run into? Terrell! Now I know Terrance is dead. When I met Terrell in that restaurant there was something off about him. I know that twins can sometimes mimic each other in a lot of ways. But today just confirmed what I was thinking!"

"Oh God, Tonya. Please don't tell me you think Terrance is alive."

"I'm not saying that, but I do think there was something off about Terrell today versus when I saw him last week. Today he was awkward and distant. At the restaurant, he was inviting and charming.

"Well, Terrell seemed anything but inviting and charming today."

"That's what I'm saying. The Terrell I met last week reminded me a lot of Terrance.

"Tonya, maybe he was in a rush, or had somewhere to be."

"I knew you would do this to me."

"Do what? Not believe you? Terrance is dead. I went to his memorial service. The man was cremated Tonya. I'm sure Shawna has his ashes in a pretty little vase somewhere in her house."

"Ok, Jamie. Maybe you are right. Maybe I am tripping."

All I knew was that something was off, and I couldn't put my finger on it just yet.

I needed to call my therapist to make light of the situation.

Shawna

I was up majority of the night thinking about Terrell and looking over numbers. I was becoming attracted to Terrell and I shouldn't be. He was Terrance's brother. Maybe I just needed some dick. Hell, I didn't know what I needed. But I knew sleeping with Terrell could end up in a disaster. I also knew that I haven't had any eight months now and something had to give. I needed to call Jamie to check back in on him with visitation for Morgan. We were still partners, but if I needed something I would just e-mail him. Just when I was about to hang up, he answered.

"Hey Shawna."

"Hey Jamie." I was twirling my hair. I didn't know what to say to him. Morgan was almost nine months. I kind of felt bad for keeping her from him this long, but I was also grieving.

"I'm sorry for not getting back to you earlier. It's been busy at the office lately."

"No, you're fine. As a matter of fact, would you be able to come over today. I want you to look over this paperwork Brian sent over. I know it's something I'm missing and it's bugging me. I also think it'll be good for you to see Morgan.

"Sure. What time?"

"Whenever you can."

"I'm on my way."

Jamie was very intelligent. It was a nagging sensation I
had inside that I couldn't shake. I knew that I was
missing something. Everything looked too good to be
true. Speak of the devil, my phone began to ring.

"Well, hello Shawna."

"Hello, Brian." I was annoyed. It was mainly because
Brian never calls me. I haven't seen him since the
funeral much less heard his voice. All of my red flags
started to go up.

"How are you?"

"What do you want Brian? Cut the small talk."

"Ok Shawna, what's up? You sent Terrell over here to
collect some paperwork from me. These accounts are so
old with no real history."

"And….your point is?"

"My point is Shawna, what are you digging for? It was
Terrance that ran your company into the ground.

I could tell he was annoyed at the fact that I requested those documents. I didn't care. It just confirmed whatever suspicion I had.

"Well he is dead now, isn't he?"

"Shawna, I'm just saying." He was trying to back pedal. We are in this together. I don't want anything but the best for our company."

"You're right Brian, I want the best for *my* company. I will call you if I need anything."

I could tell that I had gotten under Brian's skin. I didn't care. Brian knew I knew my shit, and he hated it. Terrance wasn't as smart. But if anything he knew, he knew money.

My doorbell rang. My mom was out with TJ, so I figured it was a good opportunity for Jamie to come over. I swear when I opened the door it seemed like I got wet instantly.

"Hey."

"Hey."

"Come in." I moved to the side.

"How are you?"

"I'm good."

"Look Jamie, I'm sorry that it has taken so long for me to do this." He cut me off.

"Shawna, you don't have to apologize. You were doing what you thought was right at the time. You were grieving the loss of your husband. It would have been selfish of me to demand anything of you. I wanted to give you space and time."

Damn that man knew what to say to make me forget all about why he came over in the first place.

"Jamie, I just want to say I apologize. I shouldn't have kept you from your daughter. She is in her playpen. I was going to feed her some lunch and then lay her down for a nap."

Jamie looked over towards her direction but hesitated for a moment. I could understand why he was nervous. I would be too. I followed behind him at a safe distance. When he laid eyes on Morgan, he began to tear up. He picked her up and it seemed like she knew that was her father.

"Say hi to your daddy, Morgan."

"Hi Morgan, it's finally good to meet you."

I swear it seemed like Jamie did not want to let Morgan go. He held her the entire time until she fell asleep in his arms.

"Well it seems like someone likes you."

"Yeah, well I love her. She looks just like me."

"I know."

We shared a moment of eye contact then he broke eye contact.

"What was it that you wanted me to look over?"

"Oh yeah." I handed him the papers.

I swear he looked over the papers for all of ten minutes before he caught what was wrong.

"Shawna, what account is this? Who has been managing this?"

"Brian, and supposedly Terrance."

"I'm going to tell you now, it would take someone with a great deal of knowledge to pull of this kind of embezzlement, and then to forge the paperwork like this. Someone definitely knows what they are doing."

"What do you mean?"

Jamie began explaining in detail, how the numbers didn't add up, how the paperwork had been forged somehow.

"Shawna, all I'm saying is that Terrance is smart. I won't take that from him. But his knowledge doesn't run this deep. Terrance is street smart, not Wall Street smart. From the looks of it. Someone is still embezzling money.

"I knew it. I knew it. Brian has been pissed at me since Terrance died. Supposedly Terrance was supposed to leave his share of the company to Brian, but he didn't. Brian has been pissed ever since. He called me today, and blamed everything on Terrance.

Jamie handed the papers back to me.

"Shawna just be careful. I've seen what power and money can do to a man. If he thought that he can get away with this, imagine what else he could be capable of especially if he wants the whole company.

"I know. I just don't know what to do."

Jamie and I sat, talked, and drank a few glasses of wine.

"Shawna, you know I still love you right?"

Jamie had caught me off guard. I was already horny, now I had a few drinks in me.

"I know."

He leaned over to kiss me and I didn't stop him. I began to feel all tingly inside, something I haven't felt in months.

Lisa

I didn't know what Brian was planning or what he was up to. The last week or so he has been distant. Ever since he said he would sleep with Shawna if he had to, I was on edge. I felt like if he did that. She would win. All I wanted to do was get married, have a few kids and live happily ever after. The only time Brian and I seemed to interact with each other was at work. Our home life was at a standstill. He was distant. I decided that I was going to surprise him in his office today. I usually knock when I needed to talk to him, but this time I just barged in.

"Lisa, I'm on a phone call."

"Get off." I began unzipping his pants.

"Hey look, I'm going to call you right back," he said to the other person on the phone."

I began giving him the best head he could have possibly imagined. I wanted him to think about the head he had gotten once it was over. I purposely wanted him to cum in my mouth so I could swallow. I didn't swallow often, but when I did, it meant I wanted something.

"Damn, Lisa. What was that about?"

"What?" As I was wiping the sides of my mouth.

"This!"

"I want us to stop being so distant. To stop arguing. It's almost been a week since we even spoke to each other."

"You're right Lisa, I'm sorry. I've had a lot on my mind. I know you're worried if I'm going to sleep with Shawna or not. I'm not baby. I said it because I was pissed off."

I noticed I kept hearing a phone vibrate, but it wasn't mine and it wasn't his that was on his desk.

"What's that noise?"

"What noise?"

He was playing dumb. I tried following the vibration around the office until it stopped.

"Lisa, you're being paranoid. Come back here and let me feel that pussy."

As soon as I was about to, I heard that noise again. I began following it through the office until I made it to the inside of his desk. It was another cell phone with the name Naomi popping up. I felt my heart drop into the pit of my stomach. I knew my next move had to be the smartest move.

"Why are you in my shit, Lisa?"

"Who is Naomi?"

"Naomi is work."

"Why have I never seen your work cell phone?"

"Because I keep it at work, Lisa! I don't need to take it with me everywhere except when I'm on business trips."

Brian was lying. I just didn't know about what. As far as I know he has never lied to me before today. But I could tell he was nervous about something.

"Ok." I was reluctant. But I didn't know what to do or say.

"Come here, are you going to let me fill you up inside."

I didn't want to make it seem like I had an attitude, so we fucked anyway. I wasn't into it, because I kept going back to wondering who the hell was Naomi. As long as we had been together I'd never heard of a Naomi until now. I was going to scramble my brain trying to figure it out.

"Aaaarrrgghhh." He had came and I was happy. I couldn't wait to get out of his office, so he couldn't see the attitude on my face.

He couldn't be cheating on me, could he? Was that the reason he was putting the wedding off? This couldn't be happening, maybe it was karma coming back on me for all the bad shit I wished on Shawna. I was going to get to the bottom of this Naomi person.

Brian

I'd called Shawna to pick her brain. I wanted to see how she was feeling, how she was thinking. My tone may have set her off a bit. How dare she say it's her company. It hasn't been her company in almost two years. Shawna really doesn't know who she is dealing with.

Lisa came into my office and gave me some of the best head I could possibly imagine. I was on the phone with Naomi, so it caught me off guard. I didn't know what had gotten into her. We weren't on talking terms lately, so I didn't do anything to deserve it. Whatever she did, all was forgotten at that moment. I wanted to bend Lisa over and fuck her, but Naomi kept blowing up my phone. How Lisa acted in that moment, would decide if I would stay with her. If she decided to still fuck, I would hash it out with her, if she got crazy. I knew she had to go. I didn't know what was on Lisa's mind, but I could definitely tell her demeanor had changed. We still had sex, but she was still acting funny. I made a mental note to talk to her later about it. Right now, Naomi was of importance. I needed to call her back.

"Brian! Why did you hang up on me?"

"What do you want Naomi?" She was becoming a real pain in my ass lately. She had become more demanding, and calling more. This is not what we had planned.

"You're becoming a real asshole Brian. I don't know what has gotten into you, but I need for you to tighten up."

"You still haven't told me what you wanted? When you call you always want something. What is it?"

"I need a $100,000."

"For what!?"

"Why does it matter?"

"Because it's my money!"

"Get me the money Brian. I need it before the end of the week."

"Look Naomi, I'm not giving you another dime. I already send $25,000 a month for the kids. I just brought you an Escalade truck. Now you're wanting me to send you a $100,000. You got me fucked up Naomi."

"Excuse me?" I never talked to Naomi like that. She was my soulmate. At that moment, I didn't give a fuck who she was. I was taking care of her.

"You heard me! Naomi you have to be out of your damn mind if you think I'm going to send you a $100,000 and you can't even tell me what it's for. You probably got a $100,000 sitting in an account somewhere. You just don't want to use your own money."

"Brian, you might be right. You might be wrong. But if you really want to know what I need a $100,000 for you will have to come see for yourself."

"You know what Naomi, I haven't seen the kids in a while. I might just take you up on that offer.

"See you later, Brian."

I didn't know what Naomi was up to. I felt like my life was falling apart around me. Naomi blowing up my phone. Lisa suspecting some shit. Shawna all in my ass. Terrell has also been a pain in my ass. If there was something wrong Shawna would have mentioned it by now. I felt like I was in the clear so I called my dad.

"Hey dad."

"Hey, hey Brian."

"I think everything is good. Thank you for everything."

"It's the least I could do. Let me know if you need anything else."

My dad wasn't always around, but he has been coming through lately in my adult life. I guess it was his way of making up for time that was lost. We had forged some documents, I couldn't tell the difference. So I'm sure Shawna couldn't tell the difference either.

Jamie

I was excited and nervous that Shawna was letting me see Morgan for the first time since she's been born. I never thought that I'd be a father. But seeing Morgan made my heart melt. She looked just like me and my mother. There was no way I could deny her. As bad as I wanted to be with Dana, there was no way that I would choose Dana over this beautiful baby girl.

Shawna and I shared a moment. I don't know what it was but it was a spark, something there. I didn't know how to feel or react. I didn't want to make any moves and blow my chance at ever seeing Morgan again. I felt it, so I knew she did too. I definitely didn't want Shawna to be the rebound chick. I'd just broken up with Dana earlier that morning, so I definitely didn't want to make any bad decisions. There were so many emotions that were confusing me, I didn't know what to think. I just knew at that moment, I didn't want the moment to end that I was having with Morgan. I also didn't know the right time to bring up to Shawna that Tonya was living with me. I just didn't want the moment to end with Morgan and I.

"You can feed her if you want?" I heard her soft voice speak.

"Is she eating baby food yet?"

"Nooooo, not yet. Her first tooth is coming in though, so she has been a little more fussy than normal."

I fiddled around with the bottle, I didn't really know how to hold Morgan and the bottle at the same time. It was harder than it looked on television and those baby books.

"Here, let me show you."

Shawna leaned in and showed me the correct way to hold Morgan and the bottle comfortably. It was then I knew that I loved Shawna more than anything. She was a part of my life and to move forward with her, I wanted to be honest as possible.

"Shawna, I know it's a little premature. I have something that I need to talk to you about."

"Sure, Jamie. What's it about?

"Tonya."

"What about her?" I could tell that she was annoyed.

"Well, she has been living with me since she was discharged a few months ago. I know that we've just began this visitation thing with Morgan and I don't want to complicate things. But I felt like you needed to know in case we ever do move forward with Morgan spending overnights with me."

"Really Jamie?"

"Shawna, I don't want to be dishonest with you. I feel like this is how we got here in the first place. It wouldn't be fair to you."

"I appreciate your honesty. Thank you for letting me know."

"I understand if you don't ever want to do an overnight visit with Morgan. I'd understand that."

"Jamie, let's just take baby steps first. Then we can introduce other family members."

"Thank you, Shawna for being so understanding. Even after all of this, you still have a good heart."

"It's just not about us anymore, we have a little girl to worry about."

She took that information a little better than I thought. This is what it was all about. I was a father now, something I'd never thought I'd be in a million years. But I was, and the feeling was unexplainable. I could sit here all day with Shawna if she would let me. I broke the silence between us.

"I know you probably have other things to do today. I don't want to keep you from them."

106

"You're fine Jamie! This is the first break that I've had in a long time. I know she's safe. You can stay as long as you like."

That was like music to my ears. All I wanted to do was play catch up with my daughter. I'm glad that Shawna allowed me to do just that.

Shawna

Although Jamie and I shared a moment. I had to stop
that moment. Here I was just feenin' off the scent of
Terrell, and here is Jamie. My hormones were still all
out of wack. My toys weren't cutting it anymore. I
didn't want my hormones to cloud my vision. I
definitely didn't want to sleep with Terrell, even though
at time everything about Terrell reminded me of
Terrance. Jamie, well I know Jamie and all things that
he is capable of. But I just got to a happy place in my
life where everything was calm. Jamie disclosed to me
that Tonya was living with him. I actually took the
news much better than I thought. Tonya's main concern
was always Terrance. She always thought that I was in
the way of their relationship. As fucked up as it
sounded. I could understand how she felt that way.
There was no way I was letting Morgan over there just
yet. My mommy instincts tells me that Tonya wouldn't
hurt Morgan. But history tells me that she could. I told
Jamie he could stay around as long as he liked.

"Do you mind if I go and take a shower?"

"No, sure Shawna go ahead. Morgan and I will just sit
here and play on the floor."

"Ok, TJ is with his Grandma. I'll try not to be too long.
If she gets fussy, she likes her stuffed animal and that
swingy thing."

108

"Got it."

All I wanted to do was take a nice hot bath. Something was up with Brian's shady ass, and I was destined to put my finger on it. As I was going up the stairs, I got a phone call from Terrell.

"Hey, what's up?"

"I gotta leave town for a few days."

"Why what happened?"

"Brian, he is leaving to go to California."

"He didn't tell you?"

"No!"

"Well, I'm going to peep him for a few days and see what is going on. Brian is up to something I just don't know what."

"Ok, keep me updated."

That just further confirmed my suspicions. Jamie would have told me if Brian was leaving to go to California. I own that got damn company, so I would need to know if the head is going somewhere. I was livid all over again. I jumped in the shower to clear my mind. The hot water felt good on my body. Those 15 minutes I spent in the shower were worth every minute.

I threw on my pajamas and made my way downstairs. I don't think Jamie heard me. I just observed him playing with Morgan. He seemed to be a natural at it. My mom came in with TJ. My mom already knew who Jamie was in relations to Morgan, but I had not revealed that information to TJ as of yet. I hurried downstairs.

"Hey mommy."

"Hey TJ, did you have fun?"

"Yep, look at all the cool stuff Grandma brought me."

"I see. TJ I'd like you to meet someone. This is Jamie."

"Hi, Jamie! My baby sister she gets into everything. She puts stuff in her mouth that she isn't supposed to."

"Hey little man! Yeah, I see that. She can be a handful."

Jamie looked at me as if he was hesitant in which direction he should go with the conversation. I mouthed in silence that I would talk to him later.

"Well, it's good to meet you."

"TJ go on upstairs. I'll talk to you later."

110

I didn't think it was the right time to tell TJ about Jamie. But I would in due time. He was old enough to understand, but for my own selfish reasons I hadn't told him yet.

"You need to tell that boy." My mom whispered in my ear.

"I am mom. I am. I will tonight."

"Shawna, I should go. Should I wait for you to call me, or can we set up a date so that I can see Morgan again?

"We can set up a date. I'm usually free on the weekends and you know I'm home each day. Just call before you come."

"Ok!"

Jamie and I shared a stare for a lot longer than we should have and I'm sure that my mother noticed.

"You love that man. I see the way you look at him and the way he looks at you."

"Mom, stop!"

"I've never seen you stare at Terrance the way you've stared at that man."

"Ok, mom."

My mom was right. I did love Jamie. I had plans on leaving Terrance for Jamie. That was before I found out that he was bisexual and also fucking my husband. I cared more about the fact that my now deceased husband was playing both sides than I did Jamie. I was more upset that Jamie kept it a secret and continued to sleep with us both. I didn't care about his sexual orientation. I just knew that I did love Jamie, but I didn't know how far things would go with him. I wanted to have a conversation with TJ before that conversation happened at all. I went to TJ's room where he was on his tablet.

"TJ, mommy has something that she needs to talk to you about."

"Is Uncle Terrell coming to live with us?"

"No, why would you think that?"

"He is always here, so I thought he might want to come live with us."

"No, he is just making sure that we are ok, that's all."

"Oh, well what is it mommy? Is it about that man that was here?"

"Yes...."

112

"He kinda looks like Morgan."

I froze and my mouth dried up. I didn't know what to say.

"Why do you say that?"

"They have the same color eyes and their skin is the same color."

"Well, that is what I wanted to talk to you about."

"That man, TJ, that man is Morgan's dad."

There was a long silence. I could see the wheels turning in his little head.

"Ok."

"Do you have any questions?"

"No. I kind of figured that. She looks like him."

There was no hiding that. This conversation was easier than I thought. I swear I thought this was going to be one of the hardest conversations in my life. It turned out not to be. I guess with kids, simpler is better. It's us adults that overcomplicate things.

Lisa

Brian came home as if he was in a rush. He looked pissed off and didn't even speak to me.

"Baby, everything ok?"

"Yeah, I'm good. Just a lot going on."

"Business?"

"Uh, yeah."

I had suspected Brian was cheating, because this Naomi person was still on my mind. I knew every single one of Brian's passwords. I never felt like I had to use them until now. I never thought that I would be the person on the other end trying to catch my man cheating on me. All these times I figured Shawna deserved it. Maybe this was karma coming full circle. Brian went into his office at the house and stayed there most of the night. I needed to find the time to go through his phone and bank account. I had insomnia really bad and Brian slept like a rock. I was just waiting for him to fall asleep.

I had pushed Shawna away. There was no one for me to talk to. I practically turned my back on my family for Brian. I figured I was stable even though I continued to help my mother financially.

"I'm going to bed, are you coming?"

"Nah, I'm not tired. You know I have insomnia."

"Just come to bed whenever you're ready."

Brian's voice was a little gentler than when he came in earlier. It made me second guess whether I should go through his stuff. I know once I go looking, I'm bound to find something. I just didn't know exactly what I was looking for. Brian was out in less than ten minutes. I always envied the fact that he could fall asleep so quickly.

I went into his office, and peeped around a little. Nothing out of the ordinary. I logged onto his computer. His password has pretty much been the same for eight years, he just keeps changing one number. The first thing I saw on his computer was a folder labeled "US." I clicked on it, thinking that I would find things about me and Brian. Instead there were pictures of kids and a woman. There were hundreds of pictures of them. Every so often I would scroll past a picture of him holding one of the kids. My heart started racing. This wasn't what I thought it was. Could it be? Was Brian living some type of double life? There was not one picture of us in this folder. The woman in the photos was gorgeous. She looked model like, strong cheekbones, long eyelashes. I became extremely jealous. I couldn't help but to wonder who this woman was. I stared at her pictures and the pictures of the children for a long time, and the children. There was no way that Brian could have kept this from me. I exited out of that folder. The more I looked at the pictures, the angrier I became. I scrolled down to the next file labeled "Money." There were a bunch of numbers in spreadsheets that I just assumed had to do with the business. I didn't put a lot of thought into it, until I saw the same transactions on the same day each month. I wasn't dumb, but I wasn't the brightest bulb either. I needed to figure out who this Naomi person is. I knew I wouldn't sleep until I found out who she was.

Brian

Lisa was really working my nerves lately. I'd thought about going to see Naomi and the kids but there was too much to do right here where I was. I didn't want to alarm Lisa to anything that was happening. At times, I believe that Lisa is dumb as a box of rocks. She would probably follow me to the ends of the Earth if I wanted her to. I just know I can't deal with Lisa right now. I just need to put her off a little while longer while I figure this shit out with Shawna. Then I'll figure out what Naomi is up to later. I just really wanted to go to sleep. Lisa always had insomnia so I knew I wasn't going to wait up for her tonight. I had so many things on my mind. I didn't know if I was going to fall asleep either. I needed to figure out what I was going to do about Shawna. I needed Shawna out of the picture permanently. I didn't know how I was going to do that. I had an idea that seemed absurd, but I had so much to lose if she found out that I'd been embezzling money from the company. At this point it was me or her, and I was willing to risk it all over the empire that I'd built. I had every right to feel entitled to my share of the company because it was just as much mine as it was Shawna's. I did have one other idea up my sleeve. I would draft up a negotiation between Shawna and I, which would allow me to take ownership of the company at 25%. At least, I would have some stake in the company and not feel like an employee. If I could convince her of at least that, it wouldn't be considered embezzlement, would it? I really don't want to have to resort to Plan B. Plan B required a much more thought out plan. But I would if I needed to. I would do anything for my stake in that company.

T

I felt something between Shawna and I. I didn't want to cross that line with my sister-in-law. I feel like in another life, we would have been perfect for one another. How did Terrance end up with her? She was almost too good for him even though she clearly had her flaws as well. I didn't want to make it seem like I was overstepping any boundaries with her because I do understand that Terrance and I were identical. But our personalities were not. Shawna was too good to be true, but there were too many moments where I could feel the connection. I decided to step back for a while until she needed me. My presence was starting to effect TJ and not in a good way. I didn't want to continue to confuse him although I wanted to get to know my niece and nephew.

I decided to go to a bar tonight just to take my mind off of some things. I needed to call my sisters, and let them know how I was helping Shawna out. I didn't think it would be a good time to do that right now. I knew Brian was trying to double cross Shawna, but I didn't know in what way. I felt like Shawna needed to watch her back because at this moment anything could happen. When people become desperate anything could happen. I have two more months left at my lease at this apartment, I wasn't sure if I was staying or going. If Shawna needed me to stay I would. But I sort of think that my job was done here.

I pulled up to the bar and it was very crowded. I wasn't much for large crowds but I needed a drink and part of me just didn't want to be alone to be honest. I made some small talk with the waitress and ordered some food while I watched the game. Someone comes up behind me and says in the softest voice.

"Good game huh?"

Her voice sent chills down my neck. I didn't know who it was but when I turned around, it was the other chick again.

"Oh hey…I'm sorry I forgot your name."

"It's Tonya."

"Yeeeaa.. that's right. You can sit down if you want."

I knew I could use some company in the moment. But I didn't want to confuse her in anyway."

"So you're Terrance's brother?"

"Yep."

"It's amazing, y'all must be identical."

"We are, but he was born first."

I tried not to make eye contact with her because it seemed like she was reaching for something, but I was unsure of what."

"So what are you doing here tonight?"

"Just wanted to get out, and explore the town."

"Oh, it can be pretty lively here at night. I don't get out much anymore."

She slid closer to me and put her hand on my thigh.

"I know who you really are, *Terrell.*"

"What are you talking about Tonya?"

"I *know* Terrance anywhere even if he does have a twin. I may be crazy, but I may be the only one out here that truly knows Terrance."

I began to think this chick may be really crazy like Shawna tried to warn me.

"Look Tonya, I know that you're grieving Terrance too, but I am *not* Terrance."

"Don't make me think I'm crazy *Terrell.*" She said my name with air quotes.

At that moment I knew I needed to go before this turned into me trying to prove that I wasn't Terrance.

"Tonya, I need to go. I'll see you around."

I jumped up so quick and hauled ass out of there. Shawna did tell me that she was crazy. But I didn't know what kind of crazy I'd stepped into.

Tonya

I hadn't been out in a few days. I'd been laying around the house. Jamie been moping around the house for weeks. It seems like the only happiness he had was seeing his daughter. He showed me pictures of her, and there was definitely no denying that was his kid; green eyes, curly brown hair and all. She had some of Shawna's features as well, but the resemblance mirrored Jamie. He was so sick over not being with Dana. Dana hadn't called, texted, shown up or anything. It was almost like he fell off the face of the earth. He wouldn't return any of Jamie's phone calls. The one time he did pick up the phone, him and Jamie argued for like 15 minutes until Jamie hung up on him. Jamie asked me when or if he began getting visitation with his daughter, would I be ok. I guess he inquired because of my mental instability. I know that Shawna's daughter is not Terrance's, she is my niece. I would never in a million years hurt her. I could understand why Shawna wouldn't trust me. My obsession was with Terrance and I did feel like she was in the way of all that. I still thought it may be a little premature for me to attempt to talk to her though.

I'd began seeing my therapist twice a week now instead of bi-monthly. I felt like I needed to see him because I'd ran into Terrance's twin brother, Terrell. Which I still believe was him. I know Terrance like the back of my hand. These past few weeks had me feel a little

123

unstable. I was scheduled to see my therapist today, I just really needed to talk through it and make sure that I really wasn't imagining Terrance alive instead of dead. I arrived at my therapist's office. This session was really just a check-in session. We normally meet for an hour, but this time it was just 30 minutes.

"Hello Tonya."

"Hey Dr. Robinson. I'm just only going to be here for a few. I know how you try to like to trick me into talking longer than 30 minutes."

"Tonya, no one is trying to trick you into doing anything. I just think it's good for you to communicate your thoughts."

"Ok, Dr. Robinson. I've come to terms with Terrance being dead. I got it. It messed me up a little bit to see his brother. But I just felt like deep down in my heart that it was him."

"Tonya, we've been through this before. Terrance is dead. Sometimes people experiencing severe grief can sometimes imagine a person's characteristic in other people.

"I know! I know! I haven't seen him since that one time. I'll make myself get through this Dr. R."

124

"On another note, I wanted to follow up with if you'd met your niece yet? Have you had any thoughts of harming her?"

"Of course not! She is my niece. If she was Terrance's daughter and Shawna was trying to pass her off as Jamie's then, I wouldn't know how to respond."

"Tonya, I know that you've had a lot of loss over the last few years. I want to ensure that you are ok handling a new change such as this."

"I'll be fine Dr. R. I am excited to see my niece actually. I want to talk to Shawna though. I just want to assure her that I won't hurt her or her little girl. I want Jamie to be able to have a relationship with her. I would never hurt that little girl. She is family. She is Jamie's daughter. If I hurt her, that means I would hurt Jamie, and I couldn't do that."

"Tonya, I am extremely proud of how much you have grown over the last year. You have been consistent, working through the trauma that you've experienced."

"Well Dr. R I must say, at first I was just seeing you because they made me. I feel like you have really helped me work through a lot of my pain and emotions. I needed you more than I thought.

I began to tear up, because I knew that I'd come along way. I was in such a dark place for a long time. I felt stable for the first time in my life. I felt normal. I'd do anything just to continue to stay this way. Which was part of the reason that I continue to see Dr. R.

"Tonya, I want you to do three things when you get home today, and we can meet in two weeks or three if you feel you need it. I would like for you to write down three goals for yourself and how you'd like to achieve them."

"Ok! I liked when Dr. R gave me homework. It made me have something to look forward to. I knew before I even left the office I was thinking of things, but he said only three."

"Can it be more than three?" I said excitedly.

"Sure, just a minimum of three."

"Ok!"

One goal I had in mind is that I wanted to go back to work. I needed something to do than shop, watch television and eat. I felt like I was stable enough to go back to work. I wanted to ask Jamie for a job, but I never felt like it was the right time. I would ask Jamie today. In the interim, I would just go shopping.

I found some cute shoes. I'd decided that I was going to take myself out tonight. I haven't been anywhere to meet anybody in forever. I could write that down as

126

another goal. That would be Goal #2: To meet new people. I asked Jamie if he wanted to go out with me, but he was so tied up in some work that he didn't even notice me.

"Huh, what did you say Tonya."

"Let's go out tonight."

"Not tonight Tonya, I can't. I just discovered something big!"

"Ok, no problem maybe next time."

"I'm sorry Tonya, I'll take a raincheck."

"Oh yeah, are you hiring?"

"For what?"

"Like an assistant or something?"

"Why? You want to go back to work or something?"

"Yeah, I'm thinking about it."

"I think I can create one for you if you're serious."

"Yeah, I'll run it by Shawna, I'm sure it won't be a big issue. You need something to do."

"Thanks a lot Jamie!"

.

I walked out the door, and I took a cab because I thought it may be a little easier to come back if I decided to drink. There was this bar towards downtown. It's usually packed on Fridays. I was a little nervous to go. I sat at the bar, and ordered an appetizer and a drink. There were a few guys that approached me. The dating scene was so blah. I just knew that I never wanted to do another married man that's for sure. I didn't care how charming or handsome he was. I wanted a man all to myself with no sharing. I was feeling really good about myself until I looked up and there he was sitting all by himself. I had to continue to remind myself that Terrance was dead. Terrance is dead I kept saying to myself. But that didn't keep me from approaching Terrell. Terrance was dead, maybe Terrell was my soulmate. I never saw a wedding ring. I didn't know if he had kids. To hell with it. The closer I got the more nervous I became. When I whispered in his ear. I realized this person wasn't Terrell at all. I'd met Terrell once, and felt like I've seen Terrance once. This man definitely wasn't Terrell. He smelled like Terrance, even gave me the side eye like Terrance. I didn't want to overreact in that moment, but I knew I had him spooked. I didn't know who Terrance was trying to fool, but why would he fake being dead? I was going to get to the bottom of this. There was no way I'm the one that's crazy, not again.

128

I had sobered up pretty quickly and headed to the house to tell Jamie. Jamie was still sitting in front of the computer where I'd left him.

"Jamie! Jamie!"

"Yes, Tonya! What? What happened?"

"Terrell! I mean Terrance! I mean Terrell!"

"Calm down, what about Terrell?"

"Terrance! He is alive!"

"What! Tonya, no he is dead. I went to the service."

"I know, but, but…"

I knew whatever I had to say would fall on deaf ears.

"Nevermind Jamie."

"Tonya are you ok?"

"Yeah, I'm alright."

I didn't know who else to talk to that didn't think I was crazy. I knew I would have to figure this out for myself.

"Wait, Jamie. Didn't you say Terrance was cremated?"

"Yeah, why?"

That really got the wheels to turning. Terrance was a snake and he would do anything to get out of a situation he was in. He had so much to lose. I was going to prove that he wasn't really dead, or maybe he really was dead and I was the one that was tripping.

Jamie

I'd spent so much time with Shawna over the past few weeks visiting Morgan. I think that Shawna and I were reconnecting. Morgan was getting used to seeing me as well and Shawna seemed to be in better spirits. Shawna had brought something to my attention in regards to Brian and wanted me to check it out. I didn't want to believe that Brian was doing anything shady with the company. When Mr. Johnson passed away, he told me that he only wanted Shawna and I involved. He told me on his death bed to fire anyone that had anything to do with the original company. I couldn't leave Brian high and dry. I offered him a generous severance package, but he declined. I'd decided to keep him on as a sign of good faith that he would do right by us. When Shawna told me what she thought was happening there was no way Brian could be doing any of this. It didn't take me long after sitting down and searching the accounts, that things weren't looking good. Shawna didn't have much to do with this aspect, she was really responsible for the oversight of financials. I was responsible for operations and everything down to the nitty gritty. Brian was definitely embezzling money, but to where was the real question. Shawna had access to the same programs that I did, but I think she had been out of this aspect of the business so long she may have forgotten. I ran the numbers to the accounts, and they came back. I knew these three accounts like the back of my hand. All three of those individuals had died a few years ago. The other numbers were to an offshore account. What the hell was Brian doing? I knew I needed to confront him in a way that didn't sound accusatory, but I damn sure knew he was at least embezzling money from somewhere. I was about to call Shawna and tell her until Tonya asked if I'd wanted to go to a bar with her. I was so into what was going on, I told her that I needed to take a raincheck for sure. I knew I would need a drink after this though.

I called Shawna after Tonya left to inform her because shit was about to get real.

"Hello."

"Hey Shawna, you busy?"

"No what's up.

"Well you might want to sit down for this!"

"You found something, didn't you?"

"Yeah, it's not pretty. It looks like Brian is embezzling money from some accounts where the clients have been deceased for a few years."

"I knew it! I knew it!"

"How did you know Shawna?"

"Well, I didn't know for sure, but I definitely suspected something. I just needed someone to dig deep enough to get to it."

"Terrell was definitely on to something when he starting digging, I just don't think he knew what he'd find. I definitely didn't think he would be doing anything like this."

"It wasn't making any sense Jamie. The numbers weren't adding up for some accounts that were so old but were still open. When I saw that he was overseeing these accounts, I knew something wasn't right."

"Shawna, how we are going to confront him?"

"What do you mean, how are we going to confront him? The police will be escorted up to the building to arrest him first thing in the morning. I'm not playing with Brian. I allowed him to stay because he was Terrance's friend, but this is too much."

"You're right. I definitely understand. We gave him a chance and he burned us."

"Hold on Jamie, somebody's at the door."

I waited for a little while, I heard distinctive voices in the background, one in which sounded like a male. I tried hard to hear until it got louder.

"Lisa you can leave now, I've heard enough."

"No, you don't understand. I don't know what Brian is capable of and you need to be careful."

I heard Shawna fumbling around with the phone until she picked it back up.

"Jamie, you there?"

"Yeah, I'm here. What was that about?"

"Lisa, uuugh. All of a sudden, she wants to be my friend and come over and talk as if nothing has happened. She is Morgan and TJ's godmother and she hasn't even seen them. Hell, where was she when Terrance died? But it seemed like she came to warn me about Brian. I wasn't trying to hear it though."

"You really think Brian would do something stupid?"

"No, Brian isn't built like that. He might try to bully me, but he definitely is no Terrance. I'm not worried about him."

I heard another knock at the door. But this time Shawna told me she would call me back. I guess she thought it might be Lisa again.

Lisa

After I figured out who this Naomi chick was, it was much easier for me to come to terms that Brian wasn't shit. I wasn't about to confront him on anything. What would be the point? All this time I felt like I was better than Shawna because I had the friend that wasn't a cheater and on the DL. All while he was still a liar, cheater and thief. I wanted to tell Shawna that Brian was embezzling money from the company. I wanted to be the friend and godmother she needed me to be, but after all these years of her reaching out to me and rejecting her, how could I go to her with this information? All I could do was try. I didn't know if I just really needed a friend to talk to about things that were going on with Brian or was I really trying to be a friend to Shawna. Either way I felt like she needed to know.

The whole ride to Shawna's house. I felt the anxiety building up. Would she be happy to see me or reject me the way I did her? Shawna was always so accepting of me even when I wasn't of her. It was ironic how our friendship appeared to be one-sided with me being the person that was acting bourgeois.

When I arrived, she didn't welcome me with open arms.

"Hey Shawna."

"Hey."

"Can I come in?"

"Sure."

"What do you want Lisa?"

"I can't come and visit my best friend?"

She sucked her teeth.

"Oh is that what we are? I thought best friends talk to each other and support one another. I haven't seen you in almost a year!"

"I'm sorry Shawna, I mean, I meant…."

"What do you want Lisa?"

"What?"

"It's obvious that you only come around when you're hurt emotionally or financially strapped. Which one is it? You never come around just to spend time with me and your godchildren."

Damn did I become that predictable? I hadn't been the bestest friend in the world.

136

"I just wanted to say that I'm sorry ok? I also just wanted to come and warn you about Brian."

"What about Brian?"

"I found some stuff on his computer that he has been stealing money from the company. I didn't want to believe it, but I thought you should know. I don't know what he is capable of."

"Lisa, I've heard enough. Thanks for telling me."

"Shawna, Brian hasn't been himself lately, so just be careful ok?"

"Yeah….. ok Lisa."

Even though I didn't tell her about Brian's affairs, I felt good about warning her about Brian. I wanted to go back home and pack my stuff. I wanted to leave while he wasn't there. But I thought I saw Brian's car sitting outside Shawna's house. But I could have been tripping. I've been doing that a lot lately.

I left Shawna's and stopped at the store right up the street from her house. Intuition told me not to go home just yet. Something just didn't feel right. I stuck around in the area for a little bit. I tried calling Brian but his phone went straight to voicemail.

I sat in the car just crying my eyes out feeling like I had no one and I was to blame for it.

Brian

Everybody really had me fucked up lately. Lisa, Shawna, Terrell and even that bitch Jamie. I couldn't believe Lisa was snooping through my shit. I would deal with her later but right now, I had to figure out what Shawna knew, and whether or not I would be coming clean.

I waited across the street for Lisa to leave. She probably was crying on Shawna's shoulder about the Naomi shit, and crying about how she probably wanted her friend back. Lisa was in there about 10-15 minutes. I almost missed her coming out because I just knew that she would be in there awhile. Lisa looked like she lost her best friend. Shit, Lisa did that shit a long time ago. Lisa has always been a user. She uses whatever she needs from that person to get what she wants at that time. Shawna has been known to be dismissive so I wouldn't be surprised if Shawna just sent her ass on her way.

I knocked on the door and rang the doorbell. It seemed like it took forever for Shawna to come to the door. When she did, I immediately knew what I had to do.

"Hey Shawna."

She looked like she'd seen a ghost.

"Hey Brian, what are you doing here?"

"I just wanted to come by and talk to you about some things with the company. Is it a good time?"

"Sure. You can have a seat in the kitchen."

I didn't know what was going through Shawna's mind, but I knew that I had to see what she knew. What she knew would dictate how I responded.

"Look, Shawna we are all on the same team. I know you had Terrell send for some documents on some accounts."

"Yes, I did."

"If you wanted to know all you had to do was ask Shawna. You didn't have to snoop or send Terrell on me."

"I did Brian. As a matter of fact, I did several times via e-mail, I left several messages. All of which you've never returned."

"I've been busy, just like you've been."

"I get that. But this is a company and I need to see where the money is going. Do you have anything to tell me?"

"Shawna, stop the bullshit. You already know, you just want to see how much I'm going to tell you."

"Actually, Brian. I don't know. I still haven't figured it out. All I know is those accounts are closed, but somehow there is money still coming in and out of them and they belong to you."

That was all I needed to hear to do what I needed to do. She knew way too much. There was no way I was going to lose everything to Shawna and her little bitch ass boyfriend.

"You're right, I've been managing those accounts for a while."

Shawna had gotten up because her phone had rung. I walked behind her silently and put my hands around her neck. I wanted to see the life leave her body. I watched her struggle until I heard a knock at the door. I got distracted and she elbowed me in my stomach. Shawna took off running, yelling for help.

I saw Lisa walk through the door, and I was thrown off.

"What the fuck are you doing here Lisa?"

"What are you doing here Brian? What have you done?"

"You need to get the fuck out of here Lisa now!"

Shawna came out and started yelling that she was calling the police and directed her anger at Lisa too.

"Lisa, you're in on this shit too. Brian is trying to kill me and you set me up for him to do it!"

"Shawna, I promise you, you will not get out of here alive tonight. You know too much."

"Brian, cut it out ok. This is not funny anymore. I know that you care about the business, but you've gone way too far." Lisa said.

"Lisa, stay out of this! I really wish you didn't come back, because now you're a liability."

"Brian, wait. I mean… we don't have to really do this here. I'm not on her side. I'm on yours."

I really didn't want to hear anything Lisa had to say. As far as I'm concerned she knew too much too. If I let her live then I'd have to worry about her saying something eventually. I had to think fast because now I had to deal with Lisa and Shawna. I really didn't want things to get messy, but it looks like I had no choice.

I pulled out my gun and aimed it at Lisa first. After all she was the first that needed to go.

Shawna

I couldn't believe Lisa waltzed her ass in here like we were still the best of friends. She needed me, but was no where to be found when I needed her ass at the darkest points of my life. She was my kids' godmother and she still didn't come around. I really didn't know what she wanted, but I had way too much shit on my plate to deal with her drama too.

When I heard the knock at my door I immediately thought it was Lisa and she came back. I didn't have time. But to my surprise it was Brian. Brian never came to my home, even when Terrance was alive. When he asked to come in, I felt the presence of his energy and the look in his eye told a different story. I felt like I *had* to let him in. I was home by myself. My mom had taken the kids out so that I could get some rest, but at this moment I wished she was here. When Brian asked about these accounts. I didn't want to lie, I was in my own territory and I knew my own home. I faked like my phone was going off to get away from him. But when I turned my back, I didn't know he was going to try to choke me. I felt the breath leaving my body, and there was no way I could die like this. Just as I felt like I couldn't breathe anymore, there was a knock at the door. The split second was long enough for me to elbow Brian in his stomach and take off.

I ran through the house yelling for help realizing again that I was home alone. I went into my office and grabbed my small .380 that Terrance brought some time ago for me. I thought I'd never had to use it. But he always wanted me to have one. The gun was so small, small enough to just tuck in my pants. It was going to be me or him tonight.

When I heard Lisa's voice, I automatically thought she had set me up. She'd set me up to be killed. As the conversation prolonged, I realized that she was just as afraid of Brian as I was in the moment. I didn't know what Brian was going to do, because it was two of us, unless he had a gun. The look in Brian's eye was the look of a man who had nothing to lose. I was going to try to talk him down.

"Brian, you don't have to do this. You can keep whatever you have. I just wanted to know what was happening with these accounts and the money."

"Shawna, you should have just stayed out of it. It was none of your business!"

"It was MY business, Brian! I have people that I have to answer to that are higher than me. It's not just about me or Jamie."

"That's where you're wrong Shawna, it was supposed to be MY business. You *had* to mess everything up!

Terrance was supposed to leave everything to me! It was supposed to be mine!"

I was confused. At no point did Terrance ever discuss leaving anything to Brian. Our original wills were drawn up where Terrance left everything to the family. Then right before he died, he was paranoid and left everything to me.

"What are you talking about Brian? Nothing was ever left to you. Even in the beginning. He left everything to his family before he changed everything to me."

All the color drained from Brian's face, as if he'd gotten sick to his stomach. He started pacing, hitting himself upside of his head, and talking to himself.

"You're lying Shawna! You always lie! Me and Terrance started this business from the ground up, way before you! You had to come along and mess everything up! I bet you didn't even know that he only pursued you afterwards because he found out you were the big boss of the company we were trying to merge with.

"Actually, I did Brian. Terrance and I had no secrets in the beginning, but it sounds like he kept a lot from you.

"Shut up Shawna! Just shut up!

I kept my hands close to my waist, because I was waiting for an opportunity to shoot. It seemed like the opportunity would never present itself. Someone was going to die tonight. I just hoped it wasn't me.

T

I'd been following Shawna for a while. I needed to keep an eye on her since she got everything she needed to find out what Brian had been up to. I rode past her house, and noticed two cars parked outside of her house. One which belonged to Brian. I wasn't sure of who the other one belonged to.

I got on the phone and made a phone call, because something didn't seem right.

"Hey, get over here." I hung up before they got a chance to speak.

I knew I had to proceed with caution, because from what I could tell. Brian had become a ticking time bomb lately. There was no telling what he would do or is capable of doing. I saw the door was cracked a little, but I didn't want to go in until the person I called got here. I needed back up. I was never built like Terrance, but I knew people that Terrance used to hang with. I wanted to make sure Shawna was safe. As I listened outside of the door, I heard yelling and talking. It was a little bit of Shawna and a little bit of Brian. That was all the confirmation I needed to know that Brian was in the house. I couldn't risk anything happening to Shawna. I felt a bit of spark between us, but I needed to realize that was my brother's wife. Things could never be. She probably only felt an attraction to me because of the physical resemblance that I share with Terrance.

The person I called finally drove up.

"Hey man, what's up?"

"What's going on?"

"I hear yelling and talking between Shawna and Brian."

"Have they seen you yet?

"Nope."

"Well let's break up this little party."

When I walked in, everybody looked like they'd seen a ghost. It seemed like time stopped in slow motion.

"Terrell?"

"What's up Shawna? What the hell is going on?"

"You tell me. Why Brian got a gun and why is Lisa crying?"

"Maaan you not about this life, Terrell. But he is," pointing his gun to the guy next to me.

"You're supposed to be dead. I guess I'm going to have to kill you twice then" Brian said.

"Eh look man, it's one thing that you tried to kill me, but now you trying to kill my wife. That's where I have to end it. I won't give you the opportunity to try to kill me twice."

"We were supposed to be friends, brothers. I was your family when everybody else turned their back on you. I was there for you!" Brian said.

"Man, fuck all that. This shit turned personal when I realized it was you that was trying to kill me. You tried to set me up. You snitched to the police about all of the money laundering that YOU did. Don't worry, I got some people on my payroll too. Brian you were never about this life. It pains me to know, that I'ma have to take yours. So what you about to do with that gun? Use it or put it away."

Brian looked down at his gun and raised it. But before he did, Terrance had already gave him a mean right hook, and knocked the gun right out of Brian's hand. The gun flew towards Lisa, who picked it up.

"Shoot him! Shoot him!" Brian said.

"Drop it," Shawna said.

Lisa dropped the gun and it fell where Brian could get to it. Brian and Terrance began wrestling over the gun. They both struggled until a sudden shot rang out. Everything got silent, until we realized who was hit.

Brian

I couldn't believe Shawna was really trying to convince me that Terrance didn't leave shit to me. She really didn't know how close we were. Me and Terrance were family. I treated him like family, he was the brother that I never had. It made me angry, and frustrated to feel like I've been betrayed all this time. But I felt like Shawna was fucking with me. I knew I had to end Shawna, there was no way she was getting out of this alive. I couldn't allow her to know what she knows and live. If she is gone, then the company will be all mine again. I won't have to worry about her or Terrance. I didn't want to kill Lisa either, but at this point she had become a liability. She knew too much and could put me away for life.

Lisa pleaded for her life. I couldn't allow her to guilt me into not killing her. All of this shit led back to Terrance even from the very beginning. She fucked Terrance first. She had been always jealous of Shawna and Terrance. She damned near planted the seed in my head to get Terrance out of the way. What the fuck was I doing? The more I tried to get my thoughts straight, the more Shawna talked. I found myself arguing back and forth and didn't even notice Terrell enter the house.

"Terrell, you ain't about this life man."

I thought I'd seen a ghost. I did a double take. All of a sudden I felt sick to my stomach. I couldn't breathe and the room was spinning. He is supposed to be dead. We buried him, I was at the memorial. What the fuck is going on?

Terrance said something about me trying to kill his wife, but everything he said sounded distorted, and I just got angry all over again. Terrance was my friend, my brother, my right hand man. At that moment, it was life or death and I knew that if I didn't kill him now, I wouldn't be leaving here alive either. I raised my gun to point it at him, and the hit that I felt from Terrance was enough to see the life flash before my eyes.

Terrance and I began to fight. All I could think was this is it. Everything I've ever done, all the bad shit I've ever done was coming full circle. Lisa finally had the gun. I knew she would do the right thing. I yelled to her to shoot Terrance, but she froze up. I knew I couldn't depend on her for shit. When Shawna told her to drop it. Lisa dropped the gun and I scrambled to get to it. I finally got to it and Terrance and I fought over the gun until it went off.

Everything went silent and I saw Lisa drop to the ground. I knew at that moment, I didn't have anyone or anything else that was there for me. There was a split second before I felt the heat of five bullets enter inside of my body. The burning sensation took the breath out

152

of me and I felt like I couldn't breathe. My life literally flashed before my eyes and I realized that none of it was worth it. My breathing became shallow, and the last thing I saw before I closed my eyes was looking down the barrel of the smoking gun.

Shawna

I felt like the last 20 minutes of my life had been a blur. I stared at Lisa and Brian lying on the floor in a pool of blood. I didn't know what to do.

"Shawna," Terrance whispered.

He sent chills down my spine.

"I know we don't have a lot of time, but we need to decide what we are going to do. I can get rid of both Brian and Lisa's bodies, or you can call the police and it'll just look like he tried to kill you. It's your call."

"I…I don't know Terrance. I'm going to call the police. I don't want this on my conscience.

"Ok, look I'm going to disappear. Nobody knows I'm alive except you and Terrell. I need to keep it that way for a little while. I have some more business to handle. I promise I will be back.

"No, wait Terrance don't go."

"I promise I'll be back Shawna. Just make sure you get your story straight before you call them. Tell them it was a break in. Tell them anything but that fact that I was here."

Just like that he was gone again.

I was angry at Terrell for knowing that he was alive and didn't tell me. But he offered to stay until the police arrived.

"Why didn't you tell me?" I turned to Terrell to ask him.

"It wasn't time yet."

"What do you mean?"

"It would have blown everything. Terrance couldn't let anyone know he was alive, not even you. He needed to figure out why and who was trying to kill him. Terrance wasn't paranoid or going crazy when this shit happened. I'm going to let Terrance explain everything to you. He wants to be the one to tell you the story."

"So, it's been you all this time that was around and not Terrance?"

"No, Terrance would pop up from time to time. The only person that may have saw him, may have been that crazy chick Tonya. But nobody would believe her because she is crazy. We can sort that out later. Right now, I need you to get your story straight."

"I got it, I will tell them that Brian came over to talk and then he tried to kill me when I found out he was embezzling money from my company. I'll say that he confessed to killing Terrance because he knew too. His girlfriend showed up and he shot her too."

"Ok, that sounds good Shawna. Just stick to it."

The police seemed like they arrived within a matter of minutes.

"Good Evening, Mrs. James. Can you tell me what happened here tonight?"

I stuck to what I said I was going to say. They continued to ask questions. The gun that was left at the scene, I told them that it was mine and it used to be registered to my husband. I knew Terrance would have used something he could cover up. The gun would come back to him, even though he was presumed dead.

"Well, Mrs. James, it interesting because we have been following Mr. Thompkins for a while now. He has been embezzling money all over the country. We were just waiting for an opportunity to arrest him. He was a informant for us for a long time. But I guess he got greedy."

"An informant?"

"Yes, man. Mr. Thompkins had been on our payroll for almost 15 years."

It made more and more sense. If Terrance would have found out he was a snitch earlier, Brian would have been dead. Terrance needed Brian dead for his own reasons. I became angry all over again. I needed to talk to Terrance at this point. I had to wait, but then I needed to talk to Jamie also. Since things seemed like they were getting serious with Jamie all over again. It was a long night and I needed to sleep everything off. I was so glad my mom decided to stay where she was tonight. There was no way I was sleeping alone. I had to call Jamie. My home had become a crime scene, so I needed to get a hotel.

"Hey Jamie."

"Hey, what's up?"

"I need you to come over. I have to go to a hotel tonight and I'm a nervous wreck."

"I'm coming right over."

Jamie seemed like it took forever for him to get here. My bags were already packed. I'd already booked my hotel at the Four Seasons. I needed a break.

"What the....."

"Let's go. I'll explain in the car."

We finally got in his car and drove to the hotel.

"Tonight has been a mess Jamie. I'll try to give you the condensed version of what happened tonight. Brian came over, he knew that I knew about him embezzling the money. He tried to kill me. Lisa showed up. Terrell and Terrance showed up. Brian accidentally killed Lisa and Terrance killed Brian."

"Wait, what? What do you mean Terrance? You mean in as your dead husband Terrance? Did you tell the police, he killed Brian?"

"No, it's more complicated than that. I couldn't. It's a lot Jamie. Look, I really need you right now, more than ever. I haven't talked to Terrance yet, and I don't know when I will. But I wanted to talk to you first."

We finally arrived at the hotel. I checked in and we went to our room. I really wanted Jamie to stay the night with me. But I'd understand if he didn't want to. I loved Jamie. I wanted to be with him, but I also loved my husband. I was mourning the death or supposed to be death of my husband. I didn't want to seem like I moved on too fast after him. Was I prepared to reconcile my marriage if he wanted to? Was I prepared to walk away? I didn't want to lose Jamie, but I didn't want to lose my husband either. We settled into the hotel. Jamie sat in a chair that was across from the bed. I wanted to take a shower to clear my head first before I talked with Jamie.

158

"Can I take a shower first? Then, can we talk?"

"Uh, sure Shawna. I'll be here."

There were so many thoughts. I felt like my life was a mess. The only thing I wanted to be was happy. I wanted to be happy with my life, happy with my choices. Before I met Terrance I was happy with my life. It's not like I went looking for a man. Since I met him, my life has been a whirlwind. I didn't know what I wanted to do. Through all of this, I still had to face his infidelities. I let the hot water run all over my body. I felt like my mind was clearer than when I walked into the hotel. I knew what I needed to do. When I walked out the shower, Jamie was in the same place that I left him except he was watching television this time.

"Hey."

"Hey."

"Jamie, I really need to talk to you, and I really need you to understand where I'm coming from at this very moment."

"What's up Shawna, spit it out?"

"I love you Jamie." I blurted out. "Tonight, made me realize that life is way too short to not tell people that you love them, not to tell people how you really feel."

"Wow! Shawna, wow! I love you too. You've always known that I loved you. But I just believed that you were too scared to love me back."

"I'm broken Jamie. I've been heartbroken, hurt, and damaged. I don't know if I'm the same person you met two years ago. I don't even know who I am now. The only thing I'm sure of at this moment is that I love you. I realize life is way too short not to take chances and be with who you love. I want you to understand that if Terrance does come back in my life. I'll be asking for a divorce. Terrance's lifestyle is too much and too risky. I understand if this isn't what you want, and you don't want to move forward."

"Shawna, that isn't the case at all. We've talked about this scenario with us a million times. Are you willing to put your differences aside to deal with my sister? No matter what Shawna, Tonya is still my sister and Morgan's aunt and there is nothing you can do to change that. If we enter into a relationship, you will have to come to terms with all of this. This isn't just about us, Morgan and TJ. I can't help who my family is."

"I understand Jamie. I understand all of it. If I have to deal with Tonya so be it.

Jamie

I didn't know what to expect when Shawna called me. But it wasn't her asking me to come over so we could go to a hotel. As far as I was concerned we hadn't even returned to that point yet. When I entered her home. It was a real life crime scene. You can tell that Shawna had been crying. I didn't know what happened, but I had a feeling I was about to find out. Shawna gave me all the details about Brian and his fiancée Lisa, and how Brian found out that Shawna knew he was laundering money. All I could think was it my fault and that I shouldn't have told her. That I had put her life in danger by even telling her that. I knew Shawna could handle herself, but I didn't think she would ever have to.

What really blew my mind is when she said Terrance was alive. At first, I thought Shawna was delusional. All of us were at the same funeral. I realized that she was serious. If this was the case then Tonya was right all along. Tonya "wasn't" crazy. I remember her ranting about how she knew Terrance was alive, and Terrell was really Terrance. Here all along, he was really alive.

Shawna spilled her feelings out towards me. I loved her too. Shawna was traumatized and she was acting on impulse. Once the adrenalin wore off, she'd remember that Tonya is my sister, she'd remember that I'm bisexual and she'd remember everything that kept us from having a normal relationship. I wanted Shawna in every way, but not at this expense. I needed to make her understand that if it's going to be us. It would be just us.

"Shawna, are you sure Terrance will be ok with this?"

"He will have to be Jamie. I know our friendship/situationship began rocky also. But you're Morgan's father. I can't ignore that fact, even though I wanted to. I was wrong for avoiding you and keeping you from Morgan."

"Shawna, I don't mean just ok with this. I want you to be Mrs. Mitchell. I want you to be my wife. I know this isn't how you envisioned a proposal. If you need time to think about it. That is ok, take as long as you want."

Shawna took a deep breath and looked like she was in deep thought.

"We don't have to rush anything Jamie, let's just start over. Let's just start from the beginning and get to know one another for who we are. We know each other as business partners. We know each other as sexual associates. But we don't really *know* each other. I think that is what's important. We may find that we are not as compatible as we think."

"Shawna, I don't know about you. But you are the person I want to spend the rest of my life with. I'd never thought I'd be saying this about a woman."

"Jamie, well let's address the elephant in the room. I know that you like men as well. How would that affect our relationship. Is there a subconscious feeling to be with a man, or will you be content with being with a woman for the rest of your life?"

"My sexuality has nothing to do with who I'm committed to. I just happen to like both sexes. If you're asking, if I'm more likely to cheat on you with a man than a woman. I'm not likely to cheat at all. I'm just attracted to both sexes, there is no preference to which one. If my sexuality is going to bother you Shawna, then I don't know if this will work."

It seemed like that made her feel a little better. Often times people get things confused as if I'm going to cheat with a man. My likelihood of cheating with a man is the same if I was going to cheat with a woman. If I decided to cheat.

"No, no Jamie, that's not it. It's just different that is all. I'm not judging you for who you are. When I found out about your sexuality. I was more upset that you were fucking my husband, than I was about you being bisexual. It had nothing to do with your sexuality. But I just want to be clear on my feelings as well. Since here we are, I feel like I'm ok now."

"Let's start over them. Hi Shawna, I'm Jamie and it's nice to meet you." We both laughed

"Hi Jamie, it's nice to meet you too."
Shawna and I stared at each other which seemed like eternity. I knew at that moment things would be different.

Epilogue

Terrance

I knew I had to close some doors in my life, before I moved on to the next chapter. It was for me and them, but mainly for the people that I've hurt. I'd been living with Victor for almost a year. He taught me about being comfortable in the skin I'm in, and not denying who I really am. Victor and I connected right after the trial. I became paranoid and he was there through it all. It's been a struggle these past few months, being away from Shawna and my kids. I haven't gotten to see Morgan, but I missed TJ. I knew I couldn't come back until I got my shit together. I felt like I finally got my shit together. I called Shawna, because out of everyone, I felt like I owed the most to her. The phone rang several times, I thought she wouldn't pick up.

"Hello."

"Hey, Shawna."

Her voice sent chills up my spine.

"Can we meet some place and talk?"

"Sure, when and where?"

"Are you free today around noon?"

"Sure."

166

"Meet me at the Italian spot around the corner from you."

"I'll see you there."

I didn't know what to expect from Shawna. I expected her to curse me out. I expected her to be hurt. Most of all I expected her to not to forgive me. I knew it would take time. But again, I had to do this for me and her. I went down my list of people that I knew I needed to call and reconcile things. Then next person on my list was Tonya. I didn't want to trigger anything because I felt like she was the most fragile of all people that I fucked over throughout the years. I knew the best way for me to talk to her is face to face and in public as opposed to scheduling something over the phone. I knew her schedule like clockwork. She had therapy on Mondays, Wednesdays and Fridays, Tuesdays she would get her pedicure and manicures, Thursdays she would go shopping and to her favorite Japanese spot. I was so proud that Tonya seemed "normal." It reminded me of when I first met her. I would talk her after I talked to Shawna. Then there was Jamie. I knew I would have to walk into the firm in order to talk to him face to face. He was one of those people that I knew he had an axe to grind with me. As I sat there reflecting on the last few years of my life. I lost my best friend, my wife, my job, and have been at the lowest point of my life. But within all of that, it allowed me to find myself and who I really was.

I arrived before Shawna, because I wanted to see her walk in. She looked just as good as the first day I met her. She had a walk about her that shouted confidence and that is what I loved about her. She went to the hostess stand, and I stood up to wave her over.

"Hey."

"Hey."

I didn't know whether I should hug her or what, so we just sat down.

"How have you been?"

"To be honest Terrance, I was a wreck after you died. I was depressed, mom came to live with us. It was...... hard. TJ missed you, I missed you. It was just hard."

"I can't express to you how sorry I am. I know this wasn't the best way for me to leave my family. I had to. I had to know who was trying to set me up and trying to kill me. I know you thought I was crazy before I "died." I wasn't. But I had to die."

"No, no. I see now. In hindsight, you were going a little crazy." She laughed.

"Our lives were spiraling out of control. Someone was trying to set me up and kill me. It was a mess. I knew

168

Tonya didn't shoot me that day. I knew it was Brian, but somehow I had to prove it."

"Terrance, it's ok. I didn't know how low Brian was. I didn't even know he could be that..... evil. He just didn't seem like that kind of person."

"Well, I always knew he had it in him. He began changing over the years and not for the good. I had to go in and dig deep into my old lifestyle just to get answers. Come to find out his father is who put the hit out on me to do Brian a favor."

"His father? I thought Brian never knew his father."

"He didn't. As far as I knew. But apparently he did all this time."

"Who is his father?"

"Principal Toler."

"Principal Toler? You mean TJ's Principal?"

"Yep. Remember when I told you Toler and I went way back. Well, Brian was the reason he left the game. He was the reason that he turned his whole operation over to me. I was to make sure Brian never got involved in the game. I knew he was Brian's father, but Brian didn't. Somehow, Brian found out that was his father. I'm not exactly sure how. But, that doesn't matter now.

Brian reached out to some folks back home and used his father's name to put a hit out on me. I guess when he figured it wouldn't work. He decided he would do it himself. I just didn't know how knee-deep Lisa was involved in all of this."

"She wasn't Terrance. This was all Brian."

"Nah, Shawna. Lisa was waist high in his shit. She had everything to do with it. She even called Tonya to tell her where the baby shower was located. That is why Tonya showed up that day."

"Why Terrell?" She blurted out.

"What do you mean?"

"Why Terrell? Why did you bring him into our life? Nobody had even seen him in years."

"I knew Terrell, would look out for family. Terrell would do anything I needed him to do at the time."

"I just want you to know that this meeting isn't just about you seeking the closure that you seem to need. It's also about me too."

She reached in her purse and pulled out an envelope and handed it to me.

"It's divorce papers. It has the custodial arrangements. We both leave with what we put in. Nobody has to know anything else.

"Ok…."

"I hope that you can find the arrangements and terms amicable."

I skimmed through the custodial arrangement. I wasn't worried about Shawna and any other monetary arrangements. I would have paid her whatever she wanted.

"I only see one issue."

"What's that?"

"Why isn't Morgan listed on the custodial arrangements? I know I haven't gotten to see her yet, but it's not fair that you keep her from me."

She took a long sigh, and hung her head down. I tried to read her face.

"She isn't yours."

"What?"

It seemed like I couldn't breathe, like someone took the air out of the room."

"Look Terrance, I'm not going to sit here and pretend we were both perfect, because we weren't. I don't need a DNA test to show that Morgan isn't yours."

"Well, who is her fath…." Before I could finish my sentence I already knew.

"Nevermind, I already know."

I didn't know how to feel, but I think it was hurt. My wife, who never did anything wrong our entire marriage, now had a baby by another man. It just reminded me how fucked up our life really was. But I still felt like I needed to see it.

"Do you have pictures of her?"

"Terrance… don't make this harder on yourself."

"I just want to see her."

"Ok."

She pulled out her phone and showed me a picture of Morgan. I definitely knew by that light brown hair and green eyes, she was not my daughter. She looked almost identical to Jamie.

"Thank you for that. I know you didn't have to."

172

I signed the divorce papers. I felt like that was the least I could do for her after everything I've put her through.

"Thank you, Terrance. I thought you might put up a fight about the divorce. But I do have something else to tell you."

"No, it's the least I could do for you after all I've put you through."

"Jamie and I have decided to move forward in our relationship. I just want to be happy and move forward with my life. I know this isn't what you wanted to hear."

I clenched my jaw because after all of this, Jamie still was able to be with my now ex-wife. How could I be mad though? She was doing what was best for her. If this is what makes her happy then I'm happy.

"It's ok, we will just co-parent together. I also have some news to tell you. All of these years I haven't been honest with myself therefore, not honest with others. Victor and I have started a relationship. We live together and have been for several months. This is who I am now.

She looked taken aback, but with a sense of calmness. After all, I don't think there is nothing else I could tell her that would shock her any more than I have already.

"Ok. We will co-parent together. But I need time to re-introduce you into TJ's life.

"Ok, that is only fair. I'll wait for your call.

"It was good seeing you Terrance. You look good."

"Same, here. I'll see you later.

Tonya

I was leaving my therapy appointment. I felt like I was making progress. For the first time in my life, I felt like I was doing well mentally. I could only think this is what "normal" people must feel like. I was walking when I heard my name being called. I looked up and there he was. I knew it was Terrance, and not his brother Terrell. There was always something about his presence that stood out. I froze. I felt like I couldn't move. In therapy, this is what we've been discussing is moving forward not backwards.

"Hey Tonya."

"Hey Terrance."

"How'd you know it was me?"

"I know when it's you. Just like it was you at the bar that night."

"Noooo, that wasn't me. But that was me at that Italian restaurant you saw me at a few months ago. When we sat down together."

"I knew it! Everybody kept calling me crazy. But I knew you were alive."

"Tonya, can I talk to you for a minute. I know you probably don't want to."

"No we can talk. Talk…."

"I just want to apologize for everything I've ever done to you. Everything I put you through. It wasn't fair and it was selfish of me to do the things that I did to you. I feel like I played a huge part in your mental instability. For that I apologize."

I had tears in my eyes, because that's all I've ever wanted to hear that I wasn't crazy.

"Thank you, Terrance, for this. Thank you! But I know who may be perfect for you. I want you to be careful ok? I mean just be careful," as he looked into my eyes with this serious look.

I was confused. Was Terrance trying to play matchmaker? It was then, I saw Terrell walk up and reintroduce himself.

"This is my twin brother, Terrell. He seems to have an interest in you. I think you guys will have a lot in common.

"Wait, Terrance. What is this all about?"

"It's about me trying to make it right."

Jamie

I felt like I had been on cloud nine over the past few weeks. I'd been spending more time with Shawna and Morgan. Morgan was taking to me more, and TJ was getting used to me being around. I was still concerned with Terrance resurfacing and causing a bit of a disruption for TJ. I didn't know how that was going to be handled. I guess I would cross that bridge when we got to it. Shawna told me that Terrance signed the divorced papers two weeks ago. She told him that Morgan wasn't his daughter and it seemed to upset him. But he was ok after he saw pictures of her. I'd been staying with Shawna more and we seemed to mesh well. I planned on popping the question towards the end of the year even though I previously had an impromptu proposal. However, I didn't want to rush Shawna into anything.

We had to hire two new people since Lisa and Brian were gone. I'd been interviewing all week. I'd been interviewing all week, and I had interviews all day today. We had a temp as a receptionist. She alerted me that my next interview arrived. They were her sort of early, but it worked out.

I was looking down when he walked in.

"Hello, Jamie."

I knew that voice anywhere. I immediately looked up.

"What are you doing here?"

"I'm not going to stay long. Since we are going to be a blended family. I'm only going to bring it up once."

"I'm sorry for everything. Shawna has always deserved someone like you. You're everything that I couldn't be for her. You have a beautiful daughter together, and I have a son with her. We will be seeing each other more often then I'm sure you would like. These are the cards we were dealt."

I was taken aback by the man that was standing in front of me. This definitely was not the man that I met two years ago.

"Wow, Terrance it seemed like you've finally matured into an adult. I'm proud of you for that."

"Look man, just take care of Shawna. That's all I want to say, man to man. Shawna and I were married for eight years, we had a good marriage until the end. She is a sensitive soul, and wants nothing more than someone to love her like she loves them."

"I know. I got it. Don't worry."

Terrance turned around and walked out. That was a refreshing conversation that was overdue. He really did seem to mature.

Shawna

Although the past few weeks seemed to be a blur. I finally got the closure that I needed to move on with my life. Jamie and I had been on cloud nine. I didn't know if we were in a honeymoon period or if it was because we had already revealed the worst part of ourselves to each other. It was refreshing to have him around. I felt like I no longer needed to do it by myself. I had help two times over. I knew there would be a time that I needed to reintroduce TJ to Terrance. I wasn't sure when the time would be right. Things seemed to be looking up for everybody. I'd heard that Tonya and Terrell were dating. It seemed like Tonya finally got her Terrance after all, just a different version. Jamie and I were happy and it seemed like Terrance was happy with Victor. I had an idea, but I would discuss it with Jamie before I moved forward.

"I think I have an idea."

"What's up."

"What if we throw a big get together and invite everyone as a way to reintroduce Terrance to TJ?"

"You don't think that'll be too overstimulating for him."

"Well, I'd tell him before hand and then he will be amongst family and friends, so it won't be too awkward.

"What about just having a family dinner amongst us, and invite Terrance and possibly Victor. I just think something like a get together would be too much for TJ."

"You know what I like that idea better. That is what we will do."

I called Terrance to tell him the idea, because I felt like TJ grieved him only for him to come back alive. I didn't know how to explain his death, especially when I told TJ that he would never come back. Terrance was more receptive than I thought he would be to the idea. We had it set for the following Saturday at 1:00 p.m. Now I just had to talk to TJ.

He was playing his Nintendo DS when I called his name.

"TJ, mommy needs to talk to you ok?"

I was so nervous, it felt like my heart was going to beat out of my chest.

"Ok, about what?"

182

He never even made eye contact because he was so into the game.

"We will be having a family dinner next Saturday, with Grandma, Jamie, and another guest. It is important that you listen because I really don't know how to tell you. I need you to put the game down and look at me TJ.

"I'm listening. Who is this other person mommy?"

"Well he is was very important to us. There are a lot of unexplained things that have happened over the last year.

My heart was pounding so fast, I felt like I was sweating. I didn't know how to tell TJ.

"Oh, dad's alive. I already knew that." He said it so casually.

I was taken aback by his response.

"Wait. What? How?"

"Oh, how did I know?"

"Yeah"

"I heard you on the phone with him the other day talking about meeting up or something. At first, I thought you were talking to Uncle Terrell. But then I saw those papers you and dad signed that said y'all won't be married anymore. I'm ok with it. You don't have to be secretive anymore."

"Why didn't you tell me you knew?"

"I don't know. I was confused so I just stayed to myself until you said something."
He shrugged his shoulders and went back to playing his game."

It was easier than I imagined, but I was disappointed in how he found out. I felt like both TJ and I needed therapy. Although TJ has been resilient. I can't help but to think how much trauma he has endured. I felt hopeful about the dinner.

Terrance

Shawna invited Victor and me to a family dinner today. To say I was nervous was an understatement. Shawna discussed with me that TJ already knew I was alive. I didn't know that Tonya would be in attendance too. I was in awe of how Shawna has moved on and trying to make things work with her and Jamie. Terrell was invited, but wasn't 100 percent sure if he would be coming.

"Do I look ok?" I asked Victor.

"You look fine. Who are you trying to impress anyway, me or Shawna?"

"Baby look, I haven't seen my son in almost a year. I don't know what to think. By the way we need to talk before we go?"

"I already know Terrance, we're just friends. I know this is traumatic for TJ and he doesn't need a lot of other changes right now. We will tell him when the time is right."

I always appreciated Victor for being so understanding. That was something that I loved about him the most.

"Thank you so much, you don't know how much this means to me."

We headed to Shawna's house. It was once upon a time our home. She told me she would be selling it soon and she would be buying a new home since there are so many negative memories in that one. I was so lost in my thoughts and anxious at the same time. I didn't even notice Victor pulling into Shawna's driveway. We didn't live that far away, but it seems like we were there in two or three minutes.

Victor looked at me.

"Are you ready?"

"Yeah, ready as I'll ever be."

Toler

I watched as Terrance and Victor entered Shawna's house. I was parked across the street, hidden in the shadows in an inconspicuous car. I watched as everyone, hugged, dapped and exchanged pleasantries. I could feel the anger rising within. All of these people looked happy and alive while my son, my only flesh and blood son was dead because of them.

I started the car and slowly drove off. They had yet to feel my wrath.

As I reminisced of the memories that I had with Terrance. I would have never thought that Terrance would be the one to kill my only son. He knew how much he meant to me. I practically gave Terrance everything and this is how he treats me. I had nothing but time now.

Enjoy the preview of my upcoming book Circle of Obsession. In this standalone, Tonya thinks that she has finally found love and happiness. Is it real or is it too good to be true?

Circles of
Obsession

Prologue

I thought that I had finally found happiness, but it seemed like karma had finally caught up with me. I was sitting here in my new apartment with my daughter staring into her big brown eyes wondering how I even got here. I figured out that I loved myself more and now I had someone else depending on me. It was important that I took care of myself and my daughter now. It's weird how the universe works out, because someone that hated me almost five years ago, was now helping me get my life back together. I didn't think that would ever happen. But they say you form friendships in the unlikeliest of places. I wish I could get the five years back of my life that I missed. But now, I can only move forward.

I was scared, anxious and the thoughts were back. I had to protect my sanity at all costs because Mia was depending on me now. She was two years old, and I loved her more than anything in this world.

How did we get here? Let me tell you how.

1

When I met him five years ago, I thought I was the luckiest person in the world. He was charming, handsome, had a great career, was a great communicator and thoughtful. All of the things that you would normally look for in a significant other. I'd been single for so long that I didn't even know how to interpret any of his behaviors. My paranoia kicked in, and immediately thought it may be some sort of ulterior motive. I had barriers around my heart, and it would take chainsaws and blow torches to get through to it.

Although we had met before, we officially "met" at Shawna's dinner. Terrance introduced us two weeks ago, but I avoided him at all costs. We continued to make eye contact the entire night. It was almost creepy of how attracted I was to him. I didn't know if my attraction was because of Terrance or I was really attracted to him.

"Tonya, right?""

"Yep, that's me. I said shyly.

"I'm pretty sure you know that I am Terrance's brother if the looks didn't give away.

Wow he was funny too?

192

"Nice to "meet" you again." I was sort of shy and standoffish. The same he had been to me a few times before.

"First, I want to apologize to you for my behavior over the past few months. It was important that no one knew that Terrance was alive, so I had to keep you at a distance. I was very much intrigued by your presence."

"Is that right?"

"Absolutely!"

"Tell me more."

"I love your confidence. I can tell you play hard to get and I don't mind a challenge."

"I"ve been hurt a lot in the past. So excuse me if I'm not so welcoming of you." I cut my eye in Terrance's direction.

"Well, I'm not Terrance. I am Terrell. I can tell you that Terrance and I are nothing *alike*." He put much emphasis on nothing alike.

"How do I know that?"

"Just because we grew up in the same home, doesn't make us alike. Just because we look alike and share the same DNA does not make us alike. We both have different personalities and perceptions on how to treat the people we love."

He was laying it on thick, I didn't want to fall for him. After all the last few years have been literally hell for me.

"Well, Terrell we can exchange numbers. I hope to hear from you some time."

"I'll do more than call you, how about we schedule a proper date. There is no need in going back and forth on the phone when I have you right in front of me."

He turned the charm on big time.

"Ok then."

"Next Saturday at 8 p.m. are you free?"

"As a matter of fact, I am. I'm not on babysitting duty that weekend."

"Since we have each other's phone number now, I'll look forward to hearing from you."

His charm alone put a smile on my face.

2

Terrance and I came from the same home, same upbringing, hell we were twins. You'd think we would have some traits that were alike. However, our life paths were not the same. I went off to college. Terrance went off to the streets. We had a large family and after our mother died, our family kinda fell apart. I ran off to college and left Terrance to take care of the family. I knew if I stayed I would end up with the same fate as Terrance. I felt like I had to leave. Like the rest of the family I blamed Terrance for out little brother Daron's death. I felt like everyone was responsible for him, he was our baby brother. I knew it probably made Terrance feel like shit. The truth was he was the only one that really cared about us. He put me and my sisters through college and never asked for a dime. We didn't even call to say thank you. He never once threw it in our face. As I went back down memory lane, I wasn't in a good space when mom died, something inside of me changed and it didn't seem like it was for the better.

I went off to college. I did drugs, I partied hard. The same drugs that I turned my nose up to Terrance for selling, I was doing. I went so far away to college, I wanted to make sure that news never ever got back to Terrance. It had gotten so bad at one point, I started flunking my classes. My first two semesters were the worse semesters of my life. I knew I couldn't go back home with my ass between my legs because I'd ran away in the first place. It pained me to think that I was throwing Terrance's money away. Terrance would have never judged me like I judged him. The guilt alone made me want to do better.

I had a few girlfriends in college, but none of the relationships lasted. I knew that I wasn't ready for a relationship. I was still very immature until I met Monica. Monica was my first and only love, and the same one that broke my heart. It seemed like she understood me and I just wanted her all to myself. We met my junior year in college. We had to pair up for a political group assignment, and we so happened to choose each other. I felt like it was love at first sight.

The more we talked the more I liked her. I finally got the courage to ask her on a formal date. She turned me down, telling me that she just gotten out of a bad relationship and was healing from that. I didn't want to hear that. I wanted her to be mine. I started sending her gifts and quirky text messages to attempt to win her over. It finally worked. I was wearing her down.

"You know Terrell, I've never had anyone go out of their way to show me how much they like me."

"You wouldn't let me take you on a proper date, so I just want to show what things could be like."

196

"Well, since you put it that way. Let's go on a date."

I felt like I was the luckiest man in the world when she chose me. Monica stood about 5'6, had locs that came to the middle of her back, and was stacked. She had a body for days.

Monica and I dated the rest of our time in college. We had our moments, but she really taught me about maturity. After college, we moved in together and got our first jobs at a law firm before attending law school. I knew she was the one that I wanted to spend the rest of my life with. Unfortunately, she didn't feel the same way. She wanted to finish law school and at least get some cases under her belt before we got married. At least that's what she said, but I wasn't about to let her go that easily.

3

Out of all the relationships I had prior to Terrance.

Terrance would have been the best had he not been married to Shawna. My ex- husband and ex-boyfriend's always said I was the crazy one. But I'm sure it was because of those laced drugs that I had in college. My ex-boyfriend thought he could beat on me, while my ex-husband wanted to cheat on me. Only if Terrance were really single I felt like he would have been perfect for me. I had to retract those negative thoughts because I was finally moving forward in my life. Terrance moved on, Shawna has moved on. Everything with my hectic life is starting to look up. I hadn't seen my ex-husband in years. I didn't care as long as those alimony checks kept coming. I received $8,000/month and the stipulations were even if I did remarry, he would still pay me for the rest of my life. The only way the alimony checks could stop were if I requested it, and that is something I would never do. I would never be out of his hair. I didn't need to work, I didn't have to. All the pain my ex-husband caused me, the least I deserved was alimony.

Before I met Terrell, almost the last decade of my life seemed like something out of a movie. In and out of psychiatric hospitals, jail, and seeing a psychiatrist and

198

therapist for my mental health. It seemed like a lot to manage. One thing I could say for sure, is that I absolutely adored my niece Morgan. She was absolutely beautiful. No matter how much I didn't like Shawna, I could never hurt my niece.

Terrell seemed promising. But Terrance words resonated with me about being careful with Terrell. It was nothing that Terrance could tell me at this point that would make me feel like he had my best interest at heart.

Here I was at dinner with Terrell. He was charming just like Terrance, but I could tell he was genuine. We went to this fancy restaurant. The food was amazing.

"So tell me about you?"

"What would you like to know?"

"How come a man like you isn't taken or married?"

"I haven't found the right one yet."

"That's what they all say. You're handsome, successful, no kids, seem to have a great personality and all about your family. I can't imagine no one trying to take you off the market yet. What's wrong with you?" I laughed. But I was serious too.

"What can I say?"

He changed the subject.

"Enough about me. What is a woman like you doing single?"

"Well, I guess I just attract the wrong men, or I choose the wrong men. "

"What went wrong with you and Terrance?"

He had hit a nerve, but I was trying not to show it.

"Well, Terrance was a liar and adulterer for starters. He never told me he was married. Had I known, I would have never gotten involved with him for a long 5 years. Hell, I never even knew he had a kid."

"Damn."

"Yep, by the time I found out. I had so many feelings wrapped up in him. I was angry at his wife Shawna, him and everybody in between. Are you sure Terrance is ok with us dating?"

"I'm positive."

"Is it true that you tried to kill Shawna?"

I wasn't sure how to respond. That was one of the darkest points in my life.

"Yes, but I wasn't in a good place."
I quickly changed the subject.

"Are you ok with us dating?"

"Yeah I'm ok.

"Well enough about my brother. Like I told you before I am nothing like him. I like to go for what I want. I don't have any hidden children, no wife, no anything. You can run your own background check on me."

"I intend to." I said, with a smirk.